Praise for *Let It Destroy You*

"Reading Harriet Alida Lye's prose is to be given the delicious gift of sinking deeper into the human experience. *Let It Destroy You* offers us this gift through the remarkable story of June and August, lovers fraught with passion and tension that comes alive on the page, as their pursuits of love and science collide spectacularly. This is a story of how the atomic bomb was born, but it's also a tender and intelligent exploration of two people trying to understand who they are—and what they're capable of—through the lens of one another, and the daughter they share. Lye's singular observations about life and exquisite characterizing details tell us so much about a person, a moment, a feeling. This stunning novel cements her as one of my very favourite writers. *Let It Destroy You* is exceptional." —Ashley Audrain, international bestselling author of *The Push*

"The paradox of loneliness in marriage, the shockwave of parental love—staged against history's most devastating invention, the story of August and June Snow is a tender, anguished duet, glimmering with intelligence and grace." —Sarah Henstra, Governor General's Award–winning author of *The Red Word*

"*Let It Destroy You* is a strikingly intimate novel with profound reverberations. August and June's love feels as touching as it is cruel, and their determination to protect their daughter will remind you of the staggering potential of science and our search for those little bursts of light in our darkest hours." —Ellen Keith, bestselling author of *The Dutch Wife*

Praise for *The Honey Farm*

"An aura of mystery, faintly tinged with menace, permeates Lye's sensuous debut novel." —*Publishers Weekly*

"Each lyrical line feels like a gift left at the reader's altar. A honey-mouthed debut ruminating on creation, possession, and faith." —*Kirkus Reviews*

"With a strong command of tone and a haunting sense of atmosphere, Lye's first novel will transfix readers. At times lyrical, biblical, and other-worldly, *The Honey Farm* is a suspenseful and well-crafted story." —*Booklist*

"Mysterious, suspenseful, and unnerving, *The Honey Farm* offers a thrilling narrative that examines the distorted realities and conflicting perceptions that often exist in the quietest places." —Iain Reid, award-winning author of *We Spread*

Praise for *Natural Killer: A Memoir*

"Never have I read a more moving book on the fragile filament of life . . . Harriet Alida Lye has no truck with fantasy or faith or folderol. She is a star witness to the bloom of life that surrounds death, and her work demands access to our unsentimental hearts." —Michael Winter, award-winning author of *Into the Blizzard*

"*Natural Killer* is less a cancer memoir (though it is that) as a wise and heart-affirming reflection on the ties that bind us to one another . . . [A] truly original work of autobiography." —Lauren Elkin, author of *Flâneuse*, a *New York Times* Notable Book of 2017

"Gorgeous, brutal, a meteorite of a book. *Natural Killer* holds the sheer force and radical beauty of the miracle it depicts. . . . Lye writes with the wisdom and measure of a young Didion. To read this memoir is to be changed by it." —Claudia Dey, author of *Heartbreaker*, a *Paris Review* Staff Pick

LET IT DESTROY YOU

YOU

a novel

HARRIET ALIDA LYE

McCLELLAND & STEWART

Trade paperback edition published 2023

McClelland & Stewart and colophon are registered trademarks of
Penguin Random House Canada Limited.

Library and Archives Canada Cataloguing in Publication data
is available upon request.
ISBN: 978-0-7710-0042-3
ebook ISBN: 978-0-7710-0043-0

Cover design by Jennifer Griffiths
Interior design by Matthew Flute
Cover art: (couple) George Marks/Getty Images; (gold foil texture)
More Images/Adobe Stock; (burst) valeriya_dor/Adobe Stock; (gold flecks)
banphote/Adobe Stock
Interior art: ulimi/DigitalVision Vectors/Getty Images
Typeset in Baskerville Standard by M&S, Toronto
Printed in Canada

McClelland & Stewart,
a division of Penguin Random House Canada Limited,
a Penguin Random House Company
www.penguinrandomhouse.ca

1 2 3 4 5   27 26 25 24 23

Penguin
Random House
McCLELLAND & STEWART

For Arlo & Lucy

Do not destroy what you cannot create

—Leó Szilárd

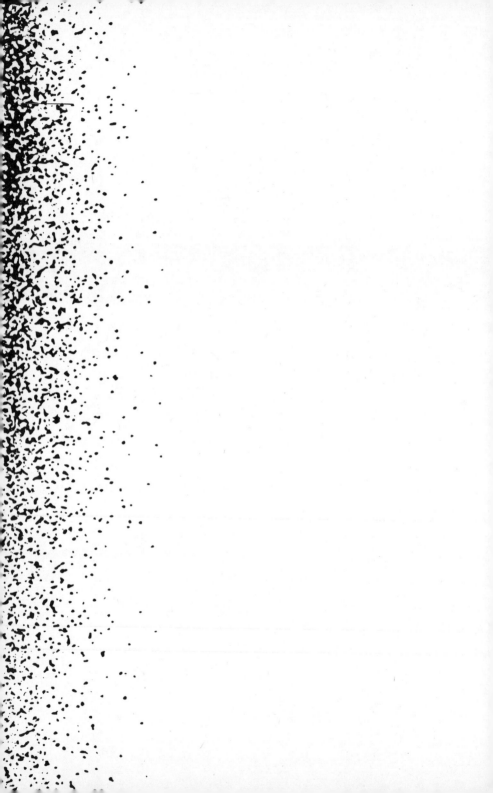

I

AUGUST

My name is August. I was born on February 11, 1898. Today is August 12, 1945, which makes me forty-seven years old. You have likely not heard of me, though there is a chance that my work has saved your life, or one day will.

I am innocent.

I stand at the window in this holding cell, watching the rolling hills in the distance disappear as night encroaches. *Encroach*—the word has always reminded me of cockroaches. I imagine the dark-black, shiny back of the Night Cockroach crawling westward, pulling his nocturnal cloak behind him. He is a few miles away yet. The sun sets late this far north; it is after nine o'clock. For the moment, the sky is a bright, deep indigo against which I can see what looks like lightly falling snow. But it is late summer, and what falls is not snow, but ash. The ash is the reason I am here. It is why they are calling me a war criminal.

I have a glass of water in my right hand—no other beverages were provided, which surprised me: I would have thought they'd want me a little dulled in the morning—and my left hand is in my pocket, turning over a nickel that the authorities neglected to confiscate. I've never known what to do with an empty hand.

In the gleam of the windowpane, I see my reflection superimposed upon the landscape. My face is like many faces; even before it was all over the papers, you would have thought I looked familiar, like someone you'd met before. The long, sloping line of my nose, the straw broom of my eyebrows, my ears sticking out like handles. My cheeks, sagged into bulldog jowls. Looking for my eyes, I notice after a few moments that they've disappeared against the sky. Funny. They must be the very same purplish blue. I turn my head side to side, observing the effect. I look hollow, or omnipotent; it's unnerving. I stare and stare, knowing the satisfaction that comes from empirical evidence, trying to find the line to show where my eyes begin and the sky ends, but cannot. Until the cockroach comes closer, the sky and I are the same.

When I was young, I wanted to be a composer. I listened mostly to Ravel, Vivaldi, Grieg. There was this lightness, a peculiar innocence to their melodies, and the way they continue to hold the power to haunt for centuries—I wanted that. Years ago, a whole lifetime ago, when I was completing my doctorate, I borrowed a two-seater plane and taught myself to fly. I'd look out the windows at the cleaving hills, the sharply rising cliffs, the staccato of evergreens in their own organic pattern, and I could hear a symphony come from the movement of it all. No, it was more than hearing, it was a sensation that was new to me; it was as though I could physically *feel* the swooping, soaring notes. I composed music with every touch of my controls, every slant of my gaze. The patterns of the mountains created the melody of my song.

It's been years since I've flown, and so my compositions have changed in nature. I'm a scientist. Or I was, until now. The judges' decision won't change my identity, but regardless of what is decided, I will certainly no longer be able to work. Already it has been difficult. Perception is everything.

Tomorrow morning, someone—perhaps the same man who dropped me here, tall and dressed entirely in white—will come to fetch me. I will walk the long, undecorated corridors in this formally neutral complex, and stand before the International Criminal Court. There will be no jury. The prosecutors will be caustic and provocative; they will, I have been warned, make this personal.

I have nothing to hide.

Some of the newspapers are making me out to be some kind of *evil genius*, as if this—what, global destruction?—was my plan all along. For the ash falling now to be simply the foreshadowing for the end of it all. Imagine! No parent could want that. I read it all, naturally, but I am rather surprised to find myself unaffected by the criticisms. I have been known to be quite vain. But all of that doesn't reflect me, after all: I am just a prism through which opinions refract. There are journalists who defend my name (just the genius, no evil), but for the most part, the ones controlling the newspapers are against me. If it was June in the public eye, it would be much worse for her.

And then I have my fans, some of whom I saw with their homemade placards on the drive in from the airport. I'd say there were at least a hundred of them, most of them younger than me. I noticed one man, dressed quite smartly, holding a sign that said *DO NOT DESTROY WHAT YOU CANNOT CREATE*, each letter a thick black brushstroke. This is a line from a speech I gave against nuclear weapons several years ago, and thus represents a rather niche and zealous fandom. I hadn't expected such a welcome; many of them must have come from a long way away. We don't know how long the trial will go on, so how long, I wonder, do they plan to stay? I imagine the families they left behind, the jobs, the sums of money they must be spending on their sad little hotel rooms—and for what? What do they expect of me? What outcome would they find the least disappointing?

My room smells of damp wool. It hasn't rained today; the dampness must be coming from the humidity of the water; though I can't see it from here, I know. The walls are grey-painted bricks, and I immediately noticed a chip in the paint revealing the rust-coloured rock beneath. The criminals who stay in this room aren't here long enough to require a fresh paint job, nor are they in a position to complain. It's a tiny room, but I've been living in hotels, or in transit, for most of my life. I can't leave, but I don't feel trapped. My mind has always been free.

I know that what you're interested in is the bomb, but I can't tell you about that without telling you about everything that came before. I may as well start at the beginning.

Children are born with an inquisitive mind, which is to say the mind of a scientist, and I assume that I became one because in some ways I remained a child. I can see myself as I was then: the same dark eyes, the same curly hair, but of a shade so dark it absorbed colour rather than presented it, unlike the bright grey I live with now. I can inhabit my young body and feel its small-ness. I can see my hands, half the size of these hands, and move them around—playing with my toys, cutting up my breaded chicken with a knife and fork. I was very sensitive and some-what high-strung. It wasn't easy for me to be around people I hadn't met before. My first years of school were especially hard.

"How will I ever know that they really *know* me?" I asked my mother, who was beautiful like a drawing from a chil-dren's book.

She said: "You'll never really know, August, you just have to try. You have to send a little boat across the water, from your island to theirs."

I tried this. I trusted her. This is what I thought of every time I met a new person for many years, until the conscious thought became so learned by my body that it was uncon-scious habit. I was the island, and I was the boat.

My mother had a way of loving us that didn't get in the way. Her love was something I never had to worry about. For all that I would give to bring her back, I am grateful she isn't here now to see what has become of me. I wouldn't be able to explain.

She used to read my brother and sister and me these tales of apocalypse, dark stories that inculcated us with a fear of the future and an addiction to truth. Her voice was so gentle but the worlds she conjured were so terrifying. Children's stories, like any religion, are trying to teach morality. Both lend themselves to terror. There are the *good* and there are the *evil*: it is black and white. I closed my eyes and followed along intently as my mother spoke, not yet knowing how to read for myself, seeing the story vividly play out on the screen of my eyelids. I learned in these stories that everything could fall apart. The parents could die, and the monsters could come out from under the bridge, and the witches could try to eat up the good children. I listened closely, because I needed to know: When this happens, what is the way to survive? It seemed to me that there could only be one way, and I needed to know the correct path.

My mother and father, Tekla and Louis, were religious. This is how the rest of the world defined them, but for me, it wasn't even secondary. I had the privilege, at the time, of not considering it at all. Hungary was welcoming to Jews, or at least more so than much of the rest of Europe at the time. We were free to worship, or not, and observe the high holidays. There were kosher delis and bakeries. But as we grew up, while the city was still accommodating, *people* started to turn against us. You might not think there's a difference. There is. The structures were in place to support us; the businesses, the synagogues, the schools were still there. Our community still had its place. But people run systems, and so this soon changed.

When my parents went out at night, to the theatre, or the opera, which they both either loved or pretended to, I could not fall asleep until they were home. I imagined all the ways they could die, and my imagination was so strong that I couldn't believe that what I'd seen in my mind wasn't real. When they finally, inevitably, always returned, I'd cling to their legs and need my mother to lie in bed next to me until my eyelids finally fell and my breath slowed into the pace of dreams. I didn't have nightmares, just vivid reconstructions of my days.

I heard my mother tell my father that I was too concerned with the abstract. But everything is abstract, or starts out that way. Love, death, fear; electricity, mornings, family; everything is purely conceptual. Then she said I had no sense of proportion, but to this I'd say that my dear mother was naïve to the vastness of evil that existed.

My family's first home was an apartment in Pest. I was born shortly after the unification of the three parts of the city, but even then, it was still considered by most to be its own town. Pest, distinct from the bourgeois Buda. The city was beautiful, as if built piece by piece by a benevolent god showing off. But I'd say it's more impressive to know that it was made not by a higher power, but with human hands.

My city was full of beauty for its own sake. Ornate sculptures on the rounded corners of buildings at the turn of a corner, carved stone; brightly painted trams running up and down the streets for as long as people were awake, which was, it seemed to me as a child, forever. Looking up, one's view of the sky was interrupted with tram lines, street lamps, smoke. I had such love for it, a childlike love that was part admiration and part fear. Fear because it was so much bigger than me, and I was afraid it would reject me.

Down by the river, where I wasn't allowed to walk by myself, the Chain Bridge to Buda looked like stone giants standing knee-deep in the water, paths of metal running into their mouths. The oil lamps on the bridge glowed copper in the dusk; the fog absorbed the light as it rolled along the Danube. My father designed bridges, but not that one, so I could appreciate it differently, with mystical reverence rather than trying to comprehend the mathematics of it. I held my mother's hand and I felt the glow, as if I were just another lamp becoming illuminated. I haven't seen my city, or my mother, since I left; sometimes my longing for both gives me an ache that feels like heartbreak and it knocks me down like a wave.

For my tenth birthday my father gave me a chemistry set and it set something off inside of me. I read the little bound book that came in the box until I had memorized its contents. There were four different types of chemical reactions. Four, only four! A whole world, and only four possibilities! What a relief, to be able to trust in science to hone the vast chaos of this world into a predictable, specific outcome!

With science, I was given a new language to describe a world that I'd always felt at least slightly at odds with. Scientists bring the invisible out of the formless and into something tangible, some sort of visible structure. We make diagrams of atoms, electrons; we make equations for speed, gravity. The experience of learning this new language was not unlike falling in love, but it's impossible for me to tell you about the fear that goes along with this kind of love. The invisible is always the hardest to believe in.

Artists render the invisible also. Think of a sculptor, making bodies emerge from stone as if discovering something that has always been there. Or a writer, who turns feelings into words on paper that you can see and hold and recognize.

For many years, long before I began working on the bomb, I had a very clear vision of what lay at the heart of the atom. I could see it from the very first time I learned of atoms: if I'd been a painter, I would have brushed black at the periphery, gradually lightening the canvas to a bright core, a heart of radiant greenish-gold. This vision consumed me. I saw it whenever I closed my eyes. It was . . . vibrant. "Vibrant" shares a Latin root with "vibrate": *vibrare*, meaning "to set in tremulous motion, to move quickly to and fro." But the Latin comes from the Proto-Indo-European word *weip*, meaning "to turn, to tremble *ecstatically*." Wave, whip. We learn something about a culture that needs to describe things that tremble ecstatically. A fish freshly caught. A lover unsated. The heart of a flame. I can see it. We are all the same culture, after all.

———

The cockroach has arrived. The night has reached the point, a soft black, where it will be unchangeable for many hours to come. My reflection is a head, here, floating in the end-less dark. The swiftly falling ash resembles the stars that it is masking. Imagine the stars spinning, spiralling at their own random will and tumbling towards the earth—this is how it would look. It really is quite beautiful. In fact, it is exactly how I thought it would look, the same colour and weight, the same deviating but direct falling pattern. Despite my horror, there is a spark of pride at this: in all my research for this experiment, I am now, against my wishes and the world's best interests, proven to be right.

A man's clarity of judgment is never very good when he is emotionally involved. This is how June and I differed: she got too involved when Leora got sick, whereas I was able to see things from a distance. All I wanted to do was save my daughter, and all June wanted was for me to stay. Neither of these wishes are ones that can be met by a compromise, but what can I say—Leora is alive. Once the verdict is in, though, I will not be able to protect them.

JUNE

I am here only as a witness. I haven't been officially summoned, but August's lawyer strongly advised that I attend the trial. *We strongly advise.* If he brings me to the stand, I will use only my first name by means of introduction. Is that allowed? I gave up my maiden name when I married August, and now that we're separated, I feel at home in neither surname. If they ask, I will say: *I am June.*

It's after nine and the sun still hasn't set. I used to love long summer evenings, but tonight I feel hot, and airless, and hungry. I sit by the window, watching the falling ash, and I worry that it is here, in this mauve hotel room, under this foreign sky, where I will be undone.

I've left a lamp on next to my side of the bed, making the inside brighter than the outside. My reflection is floating on top of the city. I sometimes forget what I look like. It's kind of like being invisible. I'm so used to staring into the face of my daughter, examining her approach to the world, that it tricks my brain into thinking that this is what faces look like—that hers is the ideal of a face—until my own face looks, I don't know, *off* somehow. There's a fluidity to my sense of self that I've felt since becoming a mother. Maybe that's closer to what I mean when I said invisible. That I can shape-shift, camouflage. That I cannot be known. My features only become pinned down when captured in photographs, which feel alien to my sense of self. In the reflection, I don't see what I know to be true from the passport photo in my purse: I have dark eyes, dark eyebrows, dark hair. There's a heaviness, an impermeability to my face; it's always made me think of an ancient stone building. As though it's the type of face that has existed forever. But looking at my face in the window, it seems as though it might blow away with a strong wind. My hair is still quite long, and I have it in a braid right now. My daughter says that braids are for queens. She's five. In the reflection I can see her sleeping behind me, starfished on the bed. The light doesn't bother her.

Like August, wherever he is, I am unable to leave my room. August will be in some sort of holding cell, I imagine, and someone will make sure to bring him to court on time. I don't know how it works. It's not like he's in jail, is it? I can't picture him trapped. He always had this wildness about him. Even when he was in one place, there was a sense that he might leave at any time.

Me, on the other hand—no matter where I've lived or visited with Leora, I've never been able to leave. Even before the separation, I lived mostly as a single mother. For the past five years, once Leora has fallen asleep, I haven't even been able to go for a walk. But you don't want to hear me talk about how motherhood is a trap.

If I could have chosen to do things differently, I would have. I never had any control of the outcome. August believes in inevitability in a different way, but to a similar end. He believes in the unseen, the mysterious. Not the divine, or at least he wouldn't put it that way. For August, it's as though he is being puppeteered by the future holding its hand over the past. Time is an epic thing for him, not comprised simply of this lifetime. I always had a hard time understanding that. For me, time is no larger than the radius of an hour. In moments of panic, it is even smaller. I can hardly believe in five minutes from now, let alone in tomorrow morning.

My outfit for the first day of the trial is hanging in the closet. I asked the concierge at the hotel to get it pressed for me when we arrived this afternoon and it was already done when we returned from dinner. It's fine, but not perfect. I thought for so long about what I should wear; I probably thought too much, because what I ended up with feels like a costume. Like I'm pretending to be a slighted mother, an innocent woman. I don't know how to be myself.

Everything I did was in reaction. That makes me sound passive, I know, but reaction is still action. What I mean to say is that I am not without regrets.

Leora and I live in a small village near Dover. We moved there just over a year ago. I chose it because I wanted something completely different, where I had no history, but someplace that was close to home. "Home." My concept of home does not match with the reality. There was nobody in Austria for me, and no house to visit, but my heart needed something, and this was what I came up with. Dover is pretty and quiet and it turns out that I love the water even more than the mountains. The endlessness, the impossibility, that's the same, but there's also something about the sea that anchors me. It's always different, in every moment. I see the water everywhere I can go; almost every room in the house has a view of the English Channel, which from here, looks as vast as an ocean. We have four fireplaces. I walk along the beach while Leora is at school, putting nice rocks in my pockets to bring home for her. We've made a little rock garden in the back. I like the white ones, she likes the dark.

It didn't take long for us to get to The Hague. We took the boat across the Channel, under the most glorious skies. It was my first time taking the ferry, and it seemed unbelievable to be able to take such a short journey and be in a whole different country. Before the white cliffs had fully receded, we could already see the shores of France and Belgium.

"Land!" Leora shouted delightedly, like a little explorer.

The winds were harsh but the sun was bright and warm. Our hair whipped about our faces. She was in front of me, within arm's reach, holding onto the railing on the deck, and then turned around to smile, checking in, just as she did when she was little—observing me to measure her own response to new situations. I nodded, smiling, and she turned her face back towards the open water, and to the country she'd never been to before.

When we arrived at the hotel in the early afternoon, Leora wanted to unpack right away. She would have happily missed dinner to get herself organized. She likes order, to know where everything belongs. When she plays with her dolls, she spends most of her time designing the "set-up"—what I might call creating the bones of the story: the home, the characters, their jobs—and then abandons play before any interaction takes place. I wonder about that. Does she lack life experience, or have no interest in it? Have I not shown her what the real world looks like?

A few hours later, I took her into town for dinner. She held my hand as we walked, which she hardly ever does anymore. It was important for me to show her a good time. I felt— nervous, almost.

"Wouldn't it be nice if Papa came to dinner?" she said, so sweetly.

"It would be nice, wouldn't it?" If the world were an entirely different place, it *would* be nice if August could be with us.

She looked up at the sky, at this sky that is both different and the same as every sky she's ever seen. A pale-yellow tram went by, making a sound louder than I'd have expected. And then, without telling me she was going to, she closed her eyes as we kept on walking. She often does this when she walks with me, I've never asked why but I can feel her joy when she does it. It reminds me of when she was a baby, so trusting that I wouldn't cause her any harm. Harm wasn't even an option.

17

She never worried I'd drop her, for example, and of course I never did. For all the worries I have about how I'm raising her, I take comfort in this facet of her personality.

When we were being seated at the restaurant, Leora chose a plush booth that could seat six. We sat opposite from one another, and she looked at the menu as if she could read. When the waiter came I ordered mussels and fries, in English, and she said the same. Not "the same," she said just what I had said, in the same intonation too: "I'll have the steamed mussels with French fries, please." She'd never even tried mussels before, but I didn't say anything. I felt very magnanimous giving her this tiny victory, letting her choose her own food — even if it was exactly what I chose. She'd eat the fries, I figured. But when our food arrived, she loved the mussels. *Loved* them. She dove in without hesitation; it was the most fun adventure, fishing for each tiny pearl of muscle within its clasping shell. "Look, Mama! I got another one!" I think it was just the energy of the night, the excitement of being in a new place, and knowing her father was nearby.

The trial has been all over the papers; people chat about it along with the weather. When I was returning home after a walk a few weeks ago, Maggie and Nick from next door were sitting in their tiny fenced-in front garden and paused their conversation to say hello, leaving room for me to join, their openness an invitation. I'd just overheard Maggie say that it was important to remember that this man had *saved lives*, and that *the destruction was merely hypothetical.* Nick scoffed loudly; I could tell he was performing for me. He is Scottish, and though he's lived down here for forty years, he has defiantly held on to his accent. *I get a feeling about him, I can't put my finger on it*, he said, *but I don't trust him. I reckon he's the kind of man who did whatever it took to become as powerful as possible.* They are about fifteen or twenty years older than I am. Maggie has let her grey hair grow long; it looked beautiful. "Morning, June," they said, smiling, waiting. It was clear that I'd heard them, that I knew what they were talking about. Everyone was talking about it, everyone had a side. I knew what was expected of me, but I let the silence go for a breath too long before nodding, "Morning," and heading up my three stone steps. I bolted the door and ran a bath.

I chose this place for the anonymity it could afford me, but after my name is in the news, everyone will know who I am.

Something finally happened in my little life—I suppose I knew it eventually would—when the letter arrived from the lawyer. In a way, getting it was a relief: I could stop waiting for it.

This one's name was Peter McCauley. Peter was new. He was, according to the newspapers, a high-profile criminal defence lawyer. If August had hired a criminal defence lawyer, did this make him a criminal? Or did it just make him well-armed? I had known August's previous lawyer well—John was someone he'd kept on retainer for various patent issues that came up. We'd had dinner with John and his wife Patricia fairly often, and they always brought their four kids, all of whom loved August. I didn't think anything of it until we had Leora and never brought her anywhere. After dinner, whether we were at a restaurant in New York or their home in New Jersey, August would get onto the floor with their kids and make himself the train track, the construction site, the trampoline. I loved him so much then. I'd be sitting with John and Patricia and look over at him, and the kids, and smile, feeling this swell of pride. I wasn't proud of *him*, it's more like I was proud of myself for having chosen him.

I opened the envelope, and the world stilled as I read:

> August requests your presence at the trial
>> bring the patent paperwork from your archives
> a hotel will be paid for
> the matter of Leora's custody   just a child
>> depending on the outcome, August will be exercising
> his parental rights to the full extent

Leora was at school, so I didn't have to put on any kind of face. I let my expression melt; my feelings formed a puddle around my feet. My insides went cold. My baby, my little duck. I had lived my whole life—well, her whole life—assuming he would never take her away from me. And now—

The day passed this way, in a liquid state, until it was time to go collect her.

Even before her diagnosis I had spent hours, as I'm sure all mothers do, almost competitively imagining all the possible ways that she might die. With each new horrible possibility,

I was trying to one-up myself, hideously; once I started, I could not stop. Falling, choking, drowning, being run over by a car. Electrocution, suffocation, tripping down the stairs. Some of the ways were more abstract but no less visceral: sometimes I'd get this feeling in my heart that something was wrong and so I'd rush to check on her, asleep in bed, and though everything was fine—she was breathing, she wasn't feverish—I then worried about whether there could be something invisible, and intangible, that was happening inside of her, like a sudden dislocation of her soul. Why did I do it? I have thought about this. I rehearsed these fears until sensation dulled and all that was left was a lesson. A lesson on how to be safe, I suppose. With these nightmare fantasies it felt like I was doing the hard work of taking the precautions that would protect her from the dangers of the world.

In all of those vivid, gory imaginings, Leora being taken was not an option. The thought of her being fine, safe, and healthy, but not with me—my mind had no traction on this. It was a void into which I could not enter, which made it a different kind of horror. The worst of all fears are the ones which are purely anticipatory, which you cannot even imagine.

Worse: Would she even choose me?

I folded the single sheet of paper back into its envelope, put it into my pocket, and went to sit down by the window. When some time had passed, I retrieved the patent documents from the box at the top of my closet, where Leora could not reach. They were in a round pink hat box and it was a square peg/round hole situation, so the sides of the pages were slightly curled up, like a scroll. I put them into the briefcase that I will bring tomorrow.

I have been up at night for weeks trying to imagine how it will play out, how the dynamics will feel. Most likely there will be no time for any kind of intimacy, not even a "hello" or "how are you." We will be on different sides of the wall. One thing I know is that, when I see him, a happiness will come to me, without my choosing to welcome it. I'm bracing myself for this. The idea embarrasses me. But he was the one who made me happy for so many years; he was the one I was always excited to see after months, or even hours, of not seeing him.

Alongside my happiness I imagine there will also be a sort of pain. Not for all that is going on now, for this is constant, a bass note to every day. Tomorrow there will be a new, sudden, jab in the heart. I can feel the edges of it now, just antici-pating it. The last time August and I saw each other, though there was anger, even hatred, there was also love. Love is not a given, now. I don't feel sad at the thought of not loving him anymore, for of this I am fairly certain, but the thought that he might not love me is—it changes everything.

There is pain, too, in suddenly being thrust back into the orbit of someone who was my gravitational pull for so many years. For almost all of my adult life. Absence dulls the feeling so that most days I don't have to think about it, but being in the same room as him again will put our timelines back together and they will be parallel, not overlapping. There is a point at which it is no longer possible to catch up to the present with someone, where a general recap is all you might be lucky to get. A "Fine thanks, and you?" This is not what I want from August. I think I would be sick if it came to that. I don't even want the intimacy of dailiness anymore; I'm not sure we ever had that. My longing for that isn't a memory so much as a fantasy. Maybe that's where the heart of the pain lies: that what I miss the most is something I never had.

The idea of feeling these kinds of pain when I see him is more humiliating than the thought that I might feel joy.

What will he say tomorrow? Will he tell the truth? I can't imagine August lying about his work, and yet if he doesn't—

It will be fine, I say sometimes to a person I've invented, a nice friend I keep in my head. *We will all be fine.* I repeat this now, to her, to myself, to August, wherever he is right now.

There's a little fridge filled with tiny bottles of alcohol that I noticed when we arrived in the room. I go over quietly to see what might be available. The shelves are full of test tube–sized bottles, the liquids a muted rainbow of yellow, amber, red. I twist off the top of a bottle of rum, pour it into the wide-bellied glass that has been placed upside down over a napkin on the polished countertop, and bring it back to my spot near the window. I open it up, just a crack, and can smell something chemical coming in on the wind. It might just be the salt from the sea. Sometimes an open window is enough to remind me that the world is larger than the limits of my own skin. I try to pull the air deep into my lungs but they don't seem able to fully inflate. The tiny molecules get stuck on the way down; I can feel each one like a bead in my throat. There's something wonderful, terrifying, about the flat vastness of water, how close it is to oblivion, and how it connects us all.

A few sips of the rum seem to stretch the time that is fitting too tightly around me. The grip loosens. I take off my socks using only my feet; having less touching my skin, that helps too.

I put my glass down and go lie next to Leora, moving her arms and turning her onto her side so that I can hold her body close. When she sleeps, she still seems like my baby, though it's impossible to imagine how a human as big as she is ever grew inside of me. I created her from nothing and she's not mine anymore. Her body has grown so long and taut, all the milky rolls of flesh gone—when did they go?—vanishing, with absolutely no mercy.

I have a dreadful sort of hope that after tomorrow, things will be different, and my brain somehow believes that different will be good even though every time change has happened to me it has left me disarmed. Change is *never* good. Change is out of my control. It's hard to say what I even want, but whatever the outcome is, I suppose things *will* be different, because the decision will put an end to this limbo, where nothing is fixed and everything is possible. I would live in this limbo forever, though, for if tomorrow takes my daughter away then please let it never come.

AUGUST

The night my colleagues and I conducted the nuclear fission experiment, the whole world became a changed place. I knew that this technology could generate clean, cheap energy, but it ended up doing much more than that. I saw the black, I saw the heart of oxidized gold I'd envisioned for so long, and the satisfaction of this vision finally materializing was completely indescribable. But that night I saw something else, too, something different to what had been driving me forward all those years.

Now, the ash is landing on everything I can see. The trees, the stone wall. I close my eyes, and it lands on everything I can imagine, too. The ocean, the flowers, hidden by the dark night, and on the hotel in which I imagine June and my daughter are sleeping. It looks peaceful, but there should not be snow in August.

The ash is the nuclear fallout resulting from the test, ordered by the prosecution, in advance of the trial. The bomb was set off yesterday on an unmanned launch boat, which will now be gone. Obliterated. The fish and plants and animals around it, gone, too. The amounts of material were reduced down to a tiny fraction of what I had defined, and then the bomb was set off in that boat well off the coast. If the bomb had been any larger, the ash would now be turning into black, radioactive rain. It is my sincere hope that the contamination will be contained within the twenty-mile radius of this virtual no man's land of international waters.

The ash on the water will kill less than it would if on land, which is a relief, but still. Not just all those fish, not just all the plants, but all the millions of microscopic elements that create life. The ripple effect will be great, and they did not ask me to consult on possible ways to mitigate that before going forth.

Life matters to me. This, I realize, is where I must prove myself to them.

I was sixteen when the Great War broke out, and from the beginning I could see exactly where it was heading. That the whole world would get involved. I told Gabor, my brother, what I thought would happen.

"Don't be ridiculous," he said.

"You'll see." And I was right.

Since people have no imagination whatsoever, they cannot imagine in peacetime that there could be war, and when the world is at war, they cannot imagine that there will ever be peace.

Hungary after the war was a changed place: the country swooped towards the right. Nothing was visible, but everything was different. I could feel it in the air. The way that strangers looked at us, with distrust, and worse. In my memory, the skies got darker then. Signs appeared on shop windows that my sister Rose was too young to read, and none of us told her why we were no longer allowed in certain places. My brother and I officially changed our religious status from "Israelite" to "Calvinist," the more accommodating of the Christian branches. We thought this would make it easier for us, but the change was purely formal. We were still recognized as Jews and treated accordingly.

In what I now see for its irony, Gabor and I fled to Germany, thinking antisemitism would be milder there. We had known nothing. It was incredibly disorienting to my sense of certainty to be so wrong about this. To be not who I thought I was.

Our parents stayed in Budapest with our sister. They told us they were not afraid, but I think they were simply more afraid of pulling up their roots and abandoning their home. I decided then: if I cannot have roots, then I shall have wings.

My father and sister eventually made it out, but my mother never did. She died of cancer in the breast. There were no viable treatments at the time. The surgeons advised that operating would be a waste of energy. I never got to talk to my mother about it. She nursed all three of us, my brother and sister and I, and it is rather awful to think of how that which gave us each life also took away hers.

When I arrived in Berlin, I enrolled for some physics classes at Humboldt and became a student of Einstein. He looked like a "good" character from a fairy tale. Bright eyes, a smile that said he knew what you really meant, and his animated mane gesticulating all over the place, reflecting his exhilaration. Achievement in the field of science requires a certain kind of sensitivity, and Albert was a man as free from vanity as I have ever seen. The way that he exalted my work, even in my undergraduate degree, shaped not just my career but my heart. Though I consider him my intellectual father, we had a lateral, collaborative relationship for many years.

In 1926, I heard about a family living in poverty in a crumbling apartment in East Berlin who had died when a seal in the tubing system in their very old refrigerator broke, and leaked methyl chloride gas through the air. It was a small news story, published deep into the local newspaper, but it was brought to my attention and it broke my heart. That could have been my family, that could have been anyone. I told Einstein about it, and he agreed we should find a solution to this problem that would be affordable, safe, and not reliant upon electricity, since many people could not afford that, or lived in places without electrical connections. Our work was already quite focused on atoms, their particular properties and structures, and I had for a long time been studying the different natures and reactions of many of them. It wasn't too long before we had invented a simple but very efficient cold box that was informed by this atomic research. It had no moving parts and all it required was a heat source and three simple, inexpensive fluids: water, ammonia, and butane. There would be no opportunity for seal failure, and no harmful chemicals were involved. I hoped people would learn about it, that it would become very popular, that it would save lives. This project felt like the beginning of my work lining up with my values. I was beginning to make the world a better place. I felt . . . alive.

I thought it might make me some money, too: I was quick to put the patent on the design, which was a habit I'd picked up recently on my brother's suggestion, to try to shore up my financial future, though my financial present was in need of help, as well. Patents, it seemed to me, were a simple, harmless gamble: sometimes they paid off. This one, though, did not yield as much as I thought it might; other, better inventions were made, and this was good, since all I wanted to do—all we wanted to do—was eliminate the economic inequality behind accidental death. If someone else could do that even more efficiently, well, then that was wonderful news.

Einstein was the one who told me, several months later, about the young men wearing swastikas emblazoned on their jackets attacking Jewish students on the Kurfürstendamm, striking them with sticks. Though he too was a Jew, he was more concerned about me. We both knew that his reputation would protect him.

"Be mindful of when to resist, and when to circumvent," he told me, advice I have thought of often since.

HARRIET ALIDA LYE

—

The team of Dutch scientists was instructed to create and detonate the cobalt bomb as I conceived it in order to build up the evidence against me, to illustrate the vast destruction I had imagined. And so far, it seems the experiment will be effective: the ash will contaminate every living thing it touches by the time the sun rises, according to my calculations, by which time I will be dressed in my suit and tie. The prosecution will try to use this to prove, in no uncertain terms, that I made it possible for the world to end and then profited from the inevitable.

I just used the term "scientists," but this is a word that can be rather vague, so let me make it clear exactly what I mean when I use this term generally.

A man was passing a building site, so the story goes, and asked one of the workmen what he was doing there. The workman said, "I am working for ninety cents an hour." The man turned to a second workman and asked the same question. "I am fitting bricks into this wall," said the second workman. Finally, the man turned to a third worker, and this one replied, "I am building a cathedral."

It is a very small percentage of the scientific community who are aware of the fact that they are participating in the building of cathedrals, and the people who followed the instructions for this experiment are not among them. A better word to describe them would be something like labourers, but if I'd said that, you wouldn't have understood.

I'm still calling it ash, but by now it's more like dust. Finer, more insidious. The first part of the fallout—thicker, snowflake-like, cold embers from what was burned—is quicker than what comes next, and what comes next is the most dangerous. This is what I believe will cause cancers, genetic mutations, birth defects. (I must note that while I acknowledge that my invention will *cause* cancers, I have been working on the cures. As is so often the case, the same element that destroys can also save.) The dust will be what poisons the water, flips the frogs over to float belly-up in lakes, and turns off whatever switch that makes us fertile.

As I conceived of it, pure cobalt surrounds the bomb and when detonated, the nuclear reaction changes it to Co-60, a radioactive isotope. Some call this technique a "salted bomb," which is a metaphor: to salt the earth would be to render it uninhabitable. This is the nature of the cobalt dust. My intent was not to propose that such a weapon be built, but to show that if it were, it would end human life on earth. I never tried to build one and wish that nobody ever had, or would—not even this small-scale test detonation. Tomorrow's trial is happening because I knew that people *would*. I have seen the hunger of men for war, for blood, and I have seen how the appetite for revenge is the cousin of lust.

And the people did. Governments quickly got wind of this new bomb, more terrible even than the H-bomb, and started trying to build them. It was an arms race to total oblivion. Nobody saw the irony.

I need you to understand that my patent was not on the bomb, but rather on the technology the bomb would employ. And I'm not here simply because I created it, but because I've been profiting from it. The money flowed in within months. So much of it, it was impossible to comprehend.

June had been right. She was always right.

By this point, though, I don't much care about the outcome. It will hardly affect me, not in the long run. Hiroshima is already gone. Nagasaki, too. The war has been ending for a long time and yet it goes on; perhaps it will go on forever, because of this. And now this is how I will be remembered. Not for any of the good I brought to the world, but for its final collapse.

JUNE

My life has been fairly ordinary with the exception of its proximity to August. It has been marked by tragedy, yes, but not defined by it. The man I loved, the father of my child, was the force who most shaped my path. Is this the case for all women? Maybe. But I had thought it would be different for me.

It's hard to say how August and I met, exactly, because we knew each other before we met. We learned from one another, and over time that turned into love. If histories are told well enough, we don't need romances. You could consider this a history of what came to be love. The love might not be here anymore, but it is still there, as in, back where it started. It's hard not to look back and think that our love was doomed from the start, because that's how it ended, but it didn't feel that way to live it. It felt like the most rare and special thing.

I'm feeling nostalgic now. I haven't felt like this in—I don't remember. It's late, I must be getting tired, but I doubt that I will sleep tonight.

I arrived in Berlin on August 24, 1929 with two suitcases, a scholarship to study sciences, and the name of a synagogue our rabbi knew. I was only eighteen years old and it felt incredible, almost anarchic, to move throughout my day with nobody knowing where I was at any given moment. I grew up in a small village about half a day's journey outside Vienna. I wasn't used to the feeling of the city, this constant buzzing that echoed in my body.

My mother had given me the money to buy myself a new radio since I would not be able to bring the one from home which didn't belong to me exactly, though it was primarily me who used it. I kept it tuned to the first station I found that played Mozart. His music was mathematics. It reminded me of home in the only way that didn't make me cry. Listening to it was what I imagined it would be like to swim in a lake that's the same temperature as your body. It's not that I felt sad, more like I was just hollow, and sadness was the thing that had filled up all my empty spots. I listened to it like I was searching for clues to myself. The notes lit up parts of my brain when I closed my eyes, and I tried to beam the light to the darkest places.

I went to synagogue every week. Generous families made me Shabbos dinners and asked how I was doing, really wanting to know. People were talking at synagogue. We could feel that things were bubbling up. Families had begun taking certain precautions—keeping their passports by the door, removing mezuzahs from their entryways. Berlin had a reputation for being anti-Fascist, but we knew the city would not be able to resist the rising National Socialist German Workers' Party forever.

I wore trousers, taking such grand strides down the boulevards; I saw art that didn't look like anything; heard music that sounded like a feeling. I went shopping at the KaDeWe on the Tauentzienstraße and, for the first time, bought make-up. A woman who was probably the same age as I was patiently instructed me in the most effective method of painting my face to "bring out its natural shapes," so she said, but it seemed to me that "enlivening my eyes" and "heightening my cheekbones" was in fact creating an entirely different shape as a way of diverting attention from the prehistoric drooping of my nose. I'd been vain enough to care about my appearance but lazy enough to be satisfied with the state of things, and now this young woman, my peer, was giving me the tools that would make me feel too guilty to remain idle in the face of my—not ugliness, but my overlookableness.

This woman took tweezers and a dark pencil to my eyebrows and shaped them into rounded arches above my eyes. She took a metal instrument and curled my lashes, opening up the curtains to my green eyes. *Jade*, she called them.

My lips were small, but with a different coloured pencil, peony-pink, she made them appear larger, more feminine, heightening the mountains on either side of the divot above my upper lip, which my mother always called God's fingerprint.

My cheeks she dusted with a copper powder that made them appear sculptural, and my eyelids were ringed with a thick, black, matte line. This step, more than any of the others, made me look like a different person to myself.

"Do you like it?" she asked, holding up a mirror for me to admire her work. I could tell my answer was important to her.

I thought about it. "I didn't know I could look like this."

She smiled, accepting this as a compliment. "What is it that you do?" she asked, ringing up my bill for every colour she had used in her portrait of me. It cost a fortune.

"I'm a student at the university. I study science."

She laughed. I don't know why. It wasn't patronizing.

To help pay my bills I soon got a job as a secretary in the office of the university, focusing on assisting the dean of the physics department. He knew I spoke English well, so he asked if I would be interested in translating some papers by one of the physics professors, August Snow. I said yes, of course. I would be paid a great deal more for this extra work. The dean put us in touch.

I read August's work and was blown right open. We wrote long letters back and forth. He didn't *pursue* me. It wasn't like that. He is eleven years older than me, yes, but we didn't know how old the other was when it began, or what we looked like. We didn't even know it was a beginning.

I wondered whether he was Jewish, and he asked me the same, in a delicate, roundabout way. We acknowledged it but didn't talk much about it then, other than logistics. Where, when.

The first paper I translated for August was on the law of thermodynamics. Energy cannot be created or destroyed in an isolated system. The Earth is an isolated system. All energy comes from, and must go, somewhere. It all seemed so connected to the current moment. I was riveted. He was riveting.

I enrolled as a student in one of his physics classes after finishing the translation, simply wanting to be closer to his brilliant mind. This was the first time I saw him speak, or had a chance to really look at him. I can still see that moment perfectly. I sat in the second row of the auditorium, wearing my green tweed blazer and my make-up just like I'd been taught. I felt, if not beautiful, then as beautiful as I could be.

August, Professor Snow to me then, talked about the financial crash in America, and the increasing vulnerability of the current Republic, and wove it into the research by Hertz and Franck, scientists from the Weimar Republic who had won the Nobel Prize in Physics a few years prior for their work on the impact of an electron upon an atom, and he took all of this and somehow made us all see that the people of the world might finally realize how little control they had over their lives, and how terrifying this would be, and what the role of the scientist would be in aiding this transition to what he called the "Age of Information."

August's body moved in a way I'd never seen before, as if every limb and muscle was working in sync to try to communicate an important message. Like the way delight extends all the way down to a small child's toes, every part of their body dancing independently. He wore a soft white shirt, buttoned all the way up, and had taken off his tie during the middle of a particularly impassioned part of his lecture. His figure was one of a man who spends most of his time sitting, but when he moved, he had the legerity of a bumblebee.

It might have been the shape of his eyes that made him look so permanently sad. They had a downward slope to them, almost as if they had been placed upside down. It was as if he had seen the future of the world, partly through his incredibly deep imagination but mostly through his even deeper intelligence, and he desperately wished it wasn't so bad.

I didn't think he would know who I was, but it nevertheless seemed he was happy that I was there. As he spoke in that class, even though he never looked right at me, I felt like he was performing for me. Keeping me in his vision. Making sure I was watching closely.

After the lecture was finished and all the students filtered out to their next classes, I waited in my seat, looking conspicuously through my notes, hoping he might notice me.

"You must be June." He sat down in the row in front of me and leaned his arm over the chair next to him so he could look back at me. He smelled like a father, like mashed potatoes and hard work. So. He had known. I hadn't told him I'd be taking his class, but I realized that I would have been the only new student there.

"Professor."

"Call me August."

He invited me to dinner that night, right then, and—of course—I said yes. I had the sense then that there would be nothing he could ask of me that I would refuse.

We hurried along the river to a restaurant and even though it was cold, we sat on the sidewalk terrace so that we could watch the people as they walked along the quays. I watched him and I could feel him watching me, and while we talked, it didn't matter what we talked about; we talked to fill the air, to become accustomed to one another's voices. We ate mussels and fries. I didn't realize until right now the parallel with the dinner Leora and I had tonight. Maybe there's something to that. Memory ripples and shapes the present.

"What drew you to physics, June?"

"I'm actually getting my degree in biology," I said, thinking I'd already told him this.

"I mean to my class."

I watched the way his throat moved as he swallowed his wine. Was he fishing for a compliment? I thought he would have known I was there for him. "It's all connected, isn't it," I said, at once embarrassed by my vagueness. "Honestly"—I took a breath and pulled something up from deep within myself— "I think I'm drawn to the idea that motion and behaviour can be explained according to laws, that matter always acts a certain way." I realized the truth in this for the first time as I let my thoughts go. "I've always felt as though things happen to me at random, that I'm not necessarily the one moving, but the one being moved. I thought physics might help me make sense of myself. Or if not, if that's selfish, then at least I might be able to train my mind to follow its logic and apply the same thinking to the rest of my life. To be less concerned with motivations, maybe. To just—do."

I couldn't believe how little he had said, and how simply he had unpeeled me. It was mortifying to have spoken to him in a way I had never even spoken to myself, and yet in the wake of the release I also felt the greatest relief.

"I don't think that's selfish," he said, with certainty. "Everyone's motivations are personal in some aspect, don't you think? I'm not sure I believe in pure altruism."

"What motivates you?" I felt bold.

He thought about it. He had another sip of wine. His throat did that thing. "I want the world to be a better place. I believe that science can make people safer, and wealthier, and happier."

I laughed. "That sounds so selfish."

He leaned in, brought his face close to mine. His eyes sharpened. I could smell the wine turning to vinegar on his breath. "And *I* want to be the one to do it. I want to be remembered as the man who saved the world. And that," he cleared his throat, "is not altruism."

He never treated me differently in front of other people. He had a neutral, proper way about him. For him, intimacy was also a formal thing. At times, I couldn't bear this. I wanted his love in a different way—I wanted him to love me like a fire, lighting me up, consuming me.

He took me so many places I'd never been. We'd usually walk, we loved to walk, but if it was far, or rainy, he'd order us a taxi, and he'd sit on the far side, making polite chit-chat with the driver instead of with me. He thought drivers might get lonely for conversation in their line of work.

We got caught in the rain one evening after dinner, in those early blurry days, and he invited me back to his apartment, my first time there after a month of seeing each other like this, and he ran a hot bath for us. The tub had clawed feet and a black plug on a chain. The floor in the bathroom had all sorts of mismatched green tiles, the towels white and new. I was absorbing all these details as evidence, adding more pieces to the mosaic of this man with whom I was falling in love. I had that special kind of attention that comes from being in a new place, just like travelling. My senses were heightened to the smell—lemons, soap, dust—and the sounds—running water, the hiss of the radiators warming up, snippets of conversation in the street. My body was attuned, too, to that sixth-sense kind of feeling, the awareness of another person, their body, their mood, their wants. Somehow I was able to be naked with him without thinking about the facts of our bodies, the shapes and textures; I was only aware of the heat of them.

We were together in Berlin for less than a year before I moved to Vienna for medical school. August stayed on in Germany, naturally. I was barely twenty years old. We didn't have a conversation about what would happen, whether we would stay together, whether we would write, if or when we would next see each other. It didn't seem reasonable to have these sorts of conversations with August. What happened, whatever it would be, would be inevitable.

I didn't want to be with anyone else, not really. I had other offers, but August had a way. "You can have a good man," he once said, "or you can have an interesting one." I believed him, and I wish there was a way I could explain to you how he didn't make me feel small for believing him. What I mean is, I didn't feel like a victim. He had power over me, yes, but I felt that I had my own sort of power too. He was right: I had never met anyone as interesting as him. I never thought him to be bad, though. "Bad." I don't know what that really means, in this context. He was Good, with a capital G. All the smaller scale aspects of "good," like punctuality and compliments and commitment, I learned to live without. And I sometimes felt like I was making a noble sacrifice for doing so. By allowing August to commit to his work, I really did somehow believe that I was making the world a better place. This was the infectiousness of his ego.

See! I said to the friend in my head. I could be nice to her in a way I couldn't to myself, but I had to justify myself to her sometimes, too, for I could feel her judgment. *Look what I can do! I can make sacrifices! I don't even feel any pain!*

Then three years after I left Berlin, Adolf Hitler, the leader of the Nazi party, became chancellor of Germany. His party won on a platform of violently hating people like me and August. August presumed that this antisemitism would spread, unbound by borders; he wrote to tell me that he didn't think we should stay in Europe. Despite the news, my heart leapt a little: there was a *we*. He asked if I would join him in London, England, with the plan to soon move across the ocean to the United States of America, and, though I had reservations about leaving my parents behind, when he sent me a train ticket, I left.

It was 1933. Neither of us had ever been to England before. I remember the air being so smoky, all the buildings made of stone, all the streets crowded. August liked it. I didn't. I didn't know how to do anything, and I felt so childish relying on him.

Though this was the first time we were living in the same city in years, our physical proximity made me aware of his emotional distance; he was there, but his mind floated several feet above his head. This is when my hunger for him began.

The pain of craving something you thought you already had is a difficult one to bear. I wanted him more because there was less of him to have. I was insatiable, but so was he. His hunger was not for me, though, but for that *greater good*: for discovery, and wisdom, and power. August's yearning bled into everything. Complaining felt petty, but I now believe that there is no such thing as neediness, only needs not being met.

I hid nothing from him then. I couldn't have. Any secret I thought I had, I'm sure August would know it immediately, innately—I'm sure he could see right through me.

August has always been the one to hold all the power, and tomorrow, he has the power to end me.

AUGUST

Before the idea for the bomb was my vision to generate energy from the atomic fission of specific elements, and this came to me while June and I were in London. It felt like the idea was floating around in the air, fully formed, a butterfly on the wind, and I happened to be the one who trapped it. If I hadn't been there, someone else would have instead. It felt similar to the way that music came to me when I was flying, as a young man: like the notes originated in the land, and my motion strung them together into a song.

Waiting at the crosswalk at Russell Square on the cool, dull morning of September 12, 1933, having woken up feeling rather irritable and unable to shake it, I watched the flow of cars and pedestrians, strangers maintaining a hurried rhythm, lights controlling the stop-and-go and creating channels like rivers that could be dammed up and set free, and the green never arrived to set *me* free. There was a trace of rain in the air, a fine mist, and I wondered where my walk might take me; I hoped, in any case, that it would crack open my foul mood. I liked to leave with no destination and allow the world to unfurl its plan before me. I let my mind try to catch up with and follow the movement of my surroundings, and when the light turned green—finally!—and I stepped off the curb, it seemed as though not just my mood cracked open but time itself.

I had read of students at Rutherford's lab "splitting" lithium by bombarding it with protons, and I had been fidgeting with this thought for several days and not getting anywhere, but in this moment, a true, clear thought pierced through: What if we could find an element that split into more protons and thus, somehow, keep the reaction going? Or perhaps a reaction that produced the "neutrons" which Chadwick had found? What if we could create a self-sustaining reaction— a chain reaction? The secondary neutrons produced from the splitting would surge from atom to atom, splitting apart the next nuclei one at a time until the cascade created a perpetual waterfall. We could *free* ourselves of thermodynamic laws. *Perpetual* motion. *Vast* amounts of energy. We could control atomic reactions like we control traffic!

The sunshine broke through from behind the clouds at that moment; I was bathed in gold and happily blinded. The weight which I normally carried around this world, moving like a drowsy hound, was suddenly lifted. Right now, if I jumped, I would fly. This idea could set us free from the use of coal; cities would be free of smog; releasing some of the energy within atoms would provide cheap and clean energy to the masses; this could create a new world. A new *world*! I knew that it would work the same way I knew how to breathe: this would be the most significant development in atomic science.

I envisioned my concept right through to completion on that walk, and I obtained a patent on the fission reactor the following year. I was the first in the world to do so. If anyone else tells you that they invented nuclear fission, they might be right—after all, communities across the globe simultaneously and separately came up with a concept of God—but I am the one who *won*.

This all leads to the bomb, of course, but before that, I must tell you about the atomic experiment we conducted in Chicago, in 1942, over nine years after that day in London. That was the night that we were going to create that very first human-made self-sustaining nuclear chain reaction. The Chicago Pile-1, as we were calling it, because my colleague Antonio had been calling the reactor "a crude pile of bricks and timber." Antonio was short but sturdy and had the stamina of a steam train: he just needed fuel, and then nothing could stop him from operating at maximum efficiency. He was a few years younger than me but had far less hair. His English wasn't as good as mine, either. He worked hard, yes, and I could see the excitement ignite him when it became clear that this would work, that I had been right. I don't think that his whole soul was in it, though. We differed there.

The test for the chain reaction had been booked in the calendar for months; it had been building in my mind ever since that day in London. By this point we had turned over our research to the government and so everything was very secretive. It embarrasses me to admit my naïveté, but I was still seeing this experiment as simply a test to prove my concept. Nuclear fission, clean energy; a huge leap for the field of atomic science. Though this was the beginning of the Manhattan Project, which was supported by all of the Allies, it wasn't until after the experiment's success that I could see the dark heart at the centre of it all.

When the day finally came, I woke early and walked to the special site in a basement beneath Stagg Field in the violet pre-dawn, electric streetlamps glowing the colour of fire. My brain was alive with anticipation, my mind already writing the history books about what I expected would happen. The streets were damp; there must have been a rain in the night. I looked at the trees lining the streets, planted for shade or ornamentation, and thought about how from them we've harvested lumber and made houses, bridges, pencils; from their boughs we've taken their fruit for eating, their leaves and barks for boiling into teas and medicines. As I walked, hearing my footsteps echo, I marvelled at the miracles of human ingenuity. There is nothing we cannot do.

I arrived at 6:58 a.m.

"Morning," Antonio said with a perky smile. He was, as always, wearing a perfectly tailored three-piece suit.

The lab was busy: I could feel a productive, excited energy. There were about forty-five people, maybe fifty. The group included all of the upperclassmen from my thermodynamics seminar as well as a few that had been enrolled in the class in previous years and still wanted to take part, and a few more junior physics students, as well as one German languages student I'd never met. They had all written personal letters asking if they could attend to watch, or help, whatever would get them in the room. This was a day history would be made; everyone knew it. Then, of course, there were my colleagues: Samuel Allison, Walter Zinn, Leona Woods—we called her "Hattie" and considered her a colleague though she was still just a student, only twenty-three years old. There was George Weil, and Arthur Compton, cocky ever since he'd won the Nobel back when he was thirty-five, and Herbert—Herbert Anderson. I'm sure I'm forgetting some. Every one of the people there had a purpose, and was presently executing that purpose. Wigner had been handling the design—oh, I forgot to mention him— E. P. Wigner was from Budapest, just a few years younger than I was, but enough to put us in entirely different childhood brackets and so we didn't meet until both working here, in Chicago.

"Professor?" someone called, and both Antonio and I turned our heads.

"Could you please check this?" the student asked, and both Antonio and I, moving together like passengers in the same vehicle, went to examine his work. A hierarchy, a unity, fell so naturally that it did not need to be stated. We felt like such a team, so much so that I remember noting at the time: teamwork is never as glorified as the work of an individual. I wondered who would be credited for the inevitable success of this experiment. (I wondered, but of course I hoped.) The glory of prizes, and reputation, and ambition, all of the things by which the scientific community is structured and rewarded, is at odds with the fact that there are not just teams working on projects like this together, but great succession lines that create a sort of inheritance of information. Ideas are not created in isolation.

"Looks good," Antonio confirmed. I nodded.

We were prepared. We knew exactly what we were doing. The train had already left the station.

Over the past several months, 80,590 pounds of greasy black uranium oxide powder had been packed into long blocks of graphite, which needed to be drilled in order to create the enclosure for the uranium. This was filthy, difficult work; students had worked in twelve-hour shifts round the clock. The uranium was disgusting, and I'd felt wary of it, too, knowing what had happened to Marie Curie. I didn't see why I should get my hands dirty when we had all of these students eager to be involved in this historic moment.

Everyone was in position. Hattie was on the Geiger counters, Antonio was holding the rods. The control rods had been created by nailing cadmium sheets to flat wooden strips, cadmium being a powerful neutron absorber. Samuel was standing at the ready with a bucket of a concentrated cadmium nitrate solution—in the case of an emergency runaway reaction, this would stop it instantly. There were so many possible emergencies, all of which we'd had to prepare for and justify to the National Defense Research Committee. A university campus in the middle of a densely populated American city was not an ideal place to have a nuclear meltdown.

At 16:00, I called out: "Are we ready to go?"

Everyone was silent but there was this deep, vibrating noise, like a machine starting up.

"Ready," Antonio said.

The start-up began. Walter removed the emergency control rod and secured it, remaining nearby in case he needed to return it to stop the reaction. Hattie called out the numbers from the counter in a voice that echoed throughout the entire bunker-like space, while George Weil, the only one left near the pile, gradually withdrew all but one of the cadmium rods.

Everything was going . . . fine. Perfectly. We watched.

"All right," Antonio said to George, "now, slowly, slowly, remove the last rod."

George, both hands on the giant rod, pulled it out an inch at a time.

"Leave in the final thirteen feet," I said. "What are our numbers?"

Hattie shouted them out: they were too low.

"Stop!" Antonio shouted. "We have to re-adjust for the trip levels."

"That'll take ages. Let's take a break, I'm starving." I checked my watch and it was somehow already almost eight o'clock. The day had flown by in the way that it can when immersed in something outside of yourself.

"A break?" said Hattie. "The numbers are moving!"

"I've got sandwiches," said Antonio. "Cheese and ham. We don't need to stop, we can eat them quickly and keep going."

"We're not eating sandwiches tonight," I said, patting him on the back. "Let's go out. We'll have steaks and wine. Celebrate!"

He didn't move; he looked at me with this incredulity.

I wanted to have a moment to chat with him, just the two of us. The others were fine, some had already dispersed for cigarettes outside, or brought out flasks from their pockets. It would take some time for them to remove the rods; it was a painstaking process. I brought Antonio his coat and held my umbrella as a cane, just in case. I wanted to go to the warmly lit restaurant I liked because it reminded me of the brasseries in Europe, with green leather banquettes and little round tables. June loved it there.

"All right," Antonio said, "if you insist."

We emerged from the basement underneath the football field in a bit of a stupor. I imagined the people working with us would stay on in the lab and eat their own cheese and ham sandwiches from home. Or perhaps they'd take a break and eat them sitting out on the stone steps outside, getting some fresh evening air.

When we got to the restaurant, I ordered us a nice bottle of red, something French. I didn't usually splurge like this. Of course I'd pay for Antonio, too.

"Are you happy with how it's going today?" he asked me.

I met his eye. "Antonio, a scientist should learn to phrase a question so that it does not presume an answer." The waiter finished pouring our glasses and backed away with a little bow. "Rather than ask me if I am happy, ask me how I am feeling. Do you see?"

"A wise lesson from the professor," Antonio smiled, not entirely kindly.

I pulled my napkin off the table and pressed the corner down into my collar.

"You don't like getting dirty, do you?" he said. Black smudges of graphite were embedded in his pores, on his palms, up his forearms.

"Not when I don't have to." My hands were clean. I continued as though he wasn't trying to make some larger statement, "I am happy, yes. Things are going as we had anticipated, and that is good news. I am also a bit—" I struggled to remember the word "concerned."

"Concerned?"

"We are creating something by destroying something else, and therefore it is logical to go one step forward and wonder whether this creation—so pure in intent—could not also be used in a destructive manner."

He took a large swallow of his wine. "Let's just focus on the task at hand, August," he said. "We are making clean energy. It is going well, is it not?" He nodded, trying to get me to nod too. "We can't predict the future."

"The war is getting worse, Antonio. That's not prophecy, it's in the papers."

"Even if it is, it is not our problem to solve."

"You don't think it is our responsibility? As scientists? As the creators of this machine? To make sure that it is used for good and not for . . . for that *evil*?" I couldn't help my voice from rising.

"We are speaking in abstracts, August. Whatever manipulation of this clean energy machine might occur, if it occurs, it would be arrogant to believe it is the problem of the scientist alone to resolve. It would belong to all people."

"Arrogant?" I couldn't believe this man. "This is not about ego. Do you believe a parent has no responsibility for the actions of his child? When we release this technology, is our responsibility to teach the people how to integrate it, how to manage it—our invention belongs to us as a child belongs to its parents." I looked around the room, at the people talking, eating, drinking, at the candles flickering, the sconces on the dark green walls sparkling in their cut-glass bulbs. There was a lightness to it all. These people had no idea what we were doing, or what would become of it. Neither did we.

"If this is the metaphor you want to pursue," Antonio said, "then when does a child stop belonging to its parents? If your child disobeys you, or grows up to become somehow evil, as you say, is that your fault? Is Adolf Hitler, for example, simply a reflection of his parents?"

"That's not what I'm talking about." What he said, though, punctured something that had been taking up a lot of space between us. Antisemitism was elected—not just approved, but *chosen* by the public—and I didn't know where Antonio stood on the matter. It wasn't something I was going to ask him about, but this uncertainty—this possibility of hatred—was something that I had to hold in my mind in every interaction in my life, including with my colleagues. His implication about Hitler was not off-the-cuff, and I appreciated this small but significant expression of allegiance.

I continued: "Listen. Science is politics. Whether or not you agree, that is inescapable. Weapons are far more powerful now than they were twenty, thirty years ago, but still they remain at a human scale. The war is at a turning point now. If Mr. Hitler obtained something as powerful as what we are working on now, the destruction would be worse than any one of these people," I nodded around at everyone in the restaurant, "could imagine."

He sighed. "So what do you want to do? Stop?"

"Of course not. We need to keep going, and make sure we get there first, before the Germans. Our research will help the government—"

"You trust the government?"

"I trust people. I trust people to do the right thing."

"You . . . trust people?" He seemed shocked, which quite delighted me.

I examined his face. He had a sharpness to his features: a pointy chin, a pointy nose, pointy eyebrows. His eyes were bright and dark and he observed me with a patience that surprised me. He didn't seem stupid, he didn't seem skeptical, he didn't seem spiteful. He was just—resigned. Detached, perhaps. A good scientist should be detached from the outcome of their work, with no agenda for their research, and he was a good scientist.

I could smell the steak cooking. I can't remember ever being more hungry, and yet also suddenly so un-needing of food. Perhaps my body was also was a machine I could train for efficiency.

"I do. I trust that good eventually wins. But we need to develop systems, and laws, and organizations, to ensure that it does."

When the food arrived, we ate quickly, silently, like animals over a carcass.

We returned to a lab still abuzz, and we resumed the experiment at 21:30. Everything was choreographed; it was as if we were performing a dance, a dance of the insides of a clock. George worked that final control rod again while Antonio and I stood back to monitor the neutron activity. Once again, Hattie called out the numbers. The students stood back, their work done for the moment, the work now just in the observation. Samuel was poised on the sidelines with the emergency cadmium nitrate. About an hour of this passed, time simply flying, and then—we realized that the pile had gone critical. It was self-sustaining. The moment this happened was like—it was like a plane lifting off the earth after a long runway. Complete lightness before the body shifts back with the implications of gravity. It was the 2nd of December, 1942, at 22:39.

I had done it.

My mind, which had stopped composing music for such a long time, suddenly created a series of deep chords, vibrating like an organ. The melody sounded ancient, like the earth heaving into mountains, like doom on a Biblical scale. I could feel the sound shudder throughout my whole body, like fore-shadowing.

"We did it!" I shouted.

We would still have to shut the machine down, slowly, safely, but I wasn't worried about that part. We had made the mess; we could clean it up.

E. P. opened a bottle of Chianti, which we drank from paper cups. The mood—oh, the mood of that room just then. I have never felt such a high. He took out a pen from his pocket. "Let's all sign this bottle," he said, which seemed such a funny thing to do, but then again, so does everything.

This invention would provide clean, cheap energy to the world. I knew it. We could stop tearing the land apart for coal and oil and wood. People who had been unable to access or afford electricity would now be able to keep their homes warm, their ovens on. But to understand unity is to under-stand atomization, and in the wake of this experiment I saw, too, the wake of the destruction that had been on my mind. I could picture it perfectly, almost like a memory. I saw the future, not for the first time, but now I saw it as a place where none of us would be.

JUNE

I look at Leora, who turns over in her sleep with a great big huff and repositions her stuffed elephant as a pillow. For a moment I'd forgotten she was there, here, with me. Though she has a prosthetic now, she still sleeps without it. Perhaps this is what you assumed anyway. I would have thought— well, I don't know what I'd have thought. I can imagine wanting to feel whole, but this is my own problem. Leora is whole even without the bottom of her left leg. Her right foot still fits in my hand, but it won't for much longer. I hold on to it, remembering how it felt to hold her tiny newborn foot, the size of my thumb, and remembering also the last time I saw her left foot.

If she wakes in the night, she maneuvers her way to the bathroom with a crutch, or sometimes without, if there's enough for her to hold on to. The hotel is unfamiliar to her and the bathroom is on the opposite side of the room, so I've left a pair of crutches beside the bed.

I shift her body so that I can sit on the bed beside her, and I look at her legs, the one that's there and the one that's not. Her body emits an intense, radiant heat when she sleeps. She always kicks her covers off, and before she was old enough to tell me she was too hot, I would always tuck her back in when I checked on her, thinking her feet must get cold like mine do. It's funny, in these small ways, how we assume our children are just like us, that we know what they need. We don't.

She doesn't mind if I touch what remains of her left leg, but I try not to when she's awake. It feels like a private part of her body. I don't want her to know I'm thinking about it all the time; she doesn't seem to think about it at all. I lie down next to her and can smell the soap we use at home.

As I press my nose into the back of her neck in bed, she makes a tiny little moan. My presence has probably worked its way into her dream. I hope it's not a scary one—I don't want to have turned into some monster in her dream-mind. I move her hair from her face and tuck it behind her ear. "Shh," I whisper, the sound coming before any thought. "It's all right, you're all right."

If August *exercises the full extent of his parental rights*, these words that now beat with the rhythm of my heart, would Leora miss me? Oh, I worry. But I worry more that she would not.

I have this sudden vision, so real it feels like memory, of running into my daughter, a few years older than she is now, on a busy sidewalk, her saying simply "hello," to me as she would to any acquaintance, or even a stranger. With no love at all. I feel sick.

While I used to be afraid of me dying, then of her dying, now I am so terrified of her being taken away from me. It starts with a feeling of cold in my throat that spreads to my stomach instantly. I forget about breathing. I can hear my heartbeat, which gets louder until it is all I can hear. My hands get sweaty. All fidgeting stills but my entire body feels twitchy. I'm unable to pull my thoughts away from whatever small detail on the wall I've fixated on. I'm staring now at the edge of the shadow cast by the lampshade above Leora's head, turning the mauve wall a dark lavender. Recently she asked where shadows come from, which felt like a metaphor.

Before we came to The Hague, I took the train from Dover into London to meet with a legal counsel. I didn't think I needed a lawyer—I hadn't been deposed—but I wanted advice, especially more information on patent law, and to get it in a way that meant I could remain anonymous. This was difficult, given the public nature of the case. I don't often go into London these days, but the years I spent there with August, before the war, created a mental map of the city that I will never forget. It's the only place where I feel an intuitive sense of orientation—my feet always know which way to the river.

I walked and walked, wondering what I would ask the lawyer. I arrived at the door to the building, a brown brick square, then kept on walking. I stood by the entrance to the tube for a long while, which is a good place to look as though you are purposefully waiting for something. The only people who would notice my loitering were fellow loiterers. I watched the flow of people going upstream and down, and when I got tired of looking at the people, so many faces, every one a potent mystery, I started looking at the shadows moving across the pavement instead. Several hours must have passed this way, which I realized only when I noticed how famished I was. I continued walking, my feet leading me down to the river. I ate a sandwich on a bench, and then took the train home to pick up Leora from school. The whole day had passed, and I missed her.

If she is taken away from me after tomorrow—if he takes her—

It is the worst thing he could do to me, but I would understand. I'd do the same.

You want to know about my childhood? Fine. My parents were lovely, my father a physician, my mother good at everything she did. My earliest memory is of a trip we took to the south of France. The first time I saw a palm tree it seemed like a person I'd be friends with. I was a happy child; an only child, too. I don't have much more to say about it. Memories of my own childhood dissipated, like clouds at sunset, when I had a child of my own; now it's hard for me to distinguish my experiences from hers.

I never thought I would get old. I thought I'd go from young to ancient, never this. Thirty-four is not *old*, but it's not young either. What I am referring to, really, is a loss of malleability. Motherhood created the line between people perceiving me as "becoming" and "complete." Thirty-four is meant to be an uneventful, in-between age, by which time things in a woman's life should be defined. It's the maintenance period. I'm meant to be maintaining my marriage, my home, my children's lives, and yet here I am, having unshouldered all, or many, of those responsibilities. I have a nanny now. It's strange to think that, though I have more than half of my life ahead of me—I hope— it is already on the downward slope. Maybe I should start, I don't know, volunteering.

I remember looking at myself in mirrors as a young child, pulling my cheeks, stretching my lips, widening and tightening my eyes to see how such manipulations changed me. My face was so malleable. I didn't think I ever looked the same from one day to the next. But now it has fixed. No, not fixed— in fact, it's deteriorating. If I pull the skin of my eyelids, it remains suspended for a brief moment before crinkling back into place.

Leora looks nothing like me, which is a shame many mothers have to bear, but I tolerate it particularly poorly. She has August's big owl eyes and round face, but otherwise, she is entirely her own child. If I had photos of August's parents and mine, and of their parents, then I might be able to trace the genetics across the generations and find her in family history, but as it is, we are marooned in the present. Strangers think she doesn't belong to me.

The whole journey here was so calm. She never once ran ahead of me, or dawdled getting off the boat, or complained she was hungry or tired. She read her books and looked out the window and ate and drank whatever I gave her. I expected a five-year-old to be full of sass and small rebellions, but she has a formality she must get from her father. Something about a trip often attunes her to me, too; she is always on her best behaviour when I really need it of her.

When I saw her walking towards me, on her way back from using the toilet, she didn't know I was looking at her and so I could watch her for a moment, looking out the window, looking at the people in their seats. The way her head was placed upon her neck, the way it arched forward, I don't know, there was just something so graceful and poetic about this tiny human as she stood, as she observed. The baby down on her cheeks, catching the sunlight. I could have cried. It's hard to understand this feeling. Or maybe it's not—maybe it's the easiest thing in the world—but I do find it terrifying. I made her from nothing. Well, not nothing.

How to describe to you this girl, the love of my life, so you can see her as a real person? She hears music differently; she can listen to it as though listening to a story. She doesn't rush through the things that give her pleasure in the way that I do. She can take ages building a city with her blocks and perpetually knocks it down to rebuild it, make it better. I don't know where she gets that, as living in a state of incompletion is intolerable to me.

Perhaps this is why marriage was difficult: there was no finish line except divorce. I would build something as quickly as I could and then finish, leave it there, not touch it again. If I've started something I like, I can't enjoy anything else until the thing is finished. I got like that with work, too—I could never stop. I don't like this about myself, and I love seeing Leora relish her joys so much that I don't even envy her, as I would with a friend, or with August.

She still sees the world with a . . . I don't know how else to say it but "childishness," by which I suppose I mean a curiosity: she doesn't assume she knows everything, and this creates a sense of wonder at things that truly are wonderful but which I have ceased to see. She asked me, the other day, why there were "so many circles" in the puddles. I can't remember when I stopped seeing those circles once I knew they were the ripples of raindrops.

What would she understand of the trial if I tried to explain it to her? She understands guilt insofar as she knows when she is supposed to apologize, but I think something as big as this would be too abstract for her. But what do I know: I've never tried. I attempt that impossible feat of projecting my daughter into an unimaginable future, where she is grown and independent, and I try to see what she will be like. All I've ever wanted is to bring her into the light, but what if, instead, I have cast a shadow over her life? Will she be the kind of person who can forgive me?

The war between August and I played out on her tiny body, and yet her body is more than just some symbol. Before this trip I asked her if she wanted to see her father and she said yes, she has always said yes, no hesitation. I tried to keep it open-ended for her, remind her she didn't have to make her mind up yet, but it was an uncomplicated decision for her.

"Yes, Mama." Every time. Same cadence. Polite but impatient. She still calls me Mama sometimes, when she isn't thinking about it. The rest of the time it's *Mother*.

"You don't have to, darling."

"I know. I want to."

This easy love she has for him is unbearable. I have a possessiveness of her that I wish was at least partly returned. But I can also see that this might mean I've managed to keep my own feelings out of her peripheral vision, which is what a parent is supposed to do, so perhaps I should take her attitude as a personal win.

I know I mentioned this already, but I debated for a long time what I should wear to the trial, as anyone would. It's important to make the right first impression. I don't mean on August—I mean for our public. Appearance is how we create stories. I want, for once, to be in control of my story. I decided on a gauzy white button-up blouse with no collar, a bright navy cardigan, a darker navy skirt that falls below the knee, and black pumps with only the slightest heel. A neutral, feminine lipstick. I have to look like a mother, like someone who still has to run the house, but I must also look as beautiful as I am able to, for everyone has more compassion for a beautiful woman. I must look at once uninvolved, inconvenienced, and penitent. I should not look guilty, but I should look sorry—sorry to be here, sorry that it came to this.

I decided, at the last minute, against the Star of David on the delicate gold chain. It seemed too much of a statement, and I didn't want it to say anything.

I believed I could tell this story without getting into religion, but that was green of me. Religion is what pushed us from our homes, it's what led us to America, it might also be what brought us to where we are now. You could probably make that argument.

August thinks of himself as beyond all of that, doesn't see its impact on the way he's been treated and how it changed his own behaviours and attitudes, but that's simply not the reality. I'm not saying that to absolve him. He had renounced God before I met him, and I never bothered trying to convince him that it was the rest of it—the people, this sense of a *bond*—that was more interesting. The idea of an omniscient being was the least interesting part of religion, but anyway. Faith became something private for me, which felt appropriate. More realistic. Faith is private or else it's a lie.

We fought about whether to raise Leora as Jewish. He was against it; I was lonely. In the end, he wasn't around, so I did what I wanted.

When the windows were broken and the homes painted with slurs, our privacy was taken away. We were exposed, we were hunted. This forced August into action. Then came the stars, then came the camps, then came the genocide. You know about that already. I don't want to talk about that.

I try to shake myself out of my head by moving from the bed to the window. Beyond the gate of the hotel garden, I can see, through the falling ash, that the sky is silver and the ocean is silver. The man at the desk said a storm was coming.

A vortex of clouds bends like liquid metal. It looks like something from one of the novels set in the future that August used to love. Sheets of rain hang over the skyline in the near distance, but from up here, on the eleventh floor of this hotel right beside the North Sea, no rain falls. We are in a clear patch, maybe the storm's eye, but I don't really know what the eye means. Do only hurricanes have eyes? Hurricanes and animals and potatoes.

There is a painting of a field of cornflowers hanging on the wall between the two beds; it's ambient in the way restaurant music is, and I think about how sweet it is that cornflowers are cornflower blue. It would be so much easier if everything were so simple.

I have a feeling that I want to chase, it's fleeting, moving quickly ahead of me; I want to pin it down and tell you what it's like to inhabit it. The feeling is of watching the storm, knowing it's coming for you, and then watching it pass you by.

AUGUST

There's a plain wooden chair facing the window in this room, and the intentionality of its placement seems like a joke. Someone decided at the last minute that the incarcerated should at least appreciate the view, if only from a stiff-backed cushionless seat. There is another chair in front of the small round table where I will eat breakfast tomorrow, if it is brought to me. I haven't placed any orders, so if I get anything, it will be whatever is customarily served. I can see the ash is still falling, though more delicately now. In the thick of night there is no breeze and it moves slowly, resting on the weight of the air as a feather would.

There is a clock above the door, the only door in the room, and now that the sky has reached the point where it will remain, this is the only way that I will be able to mark the passage of time until the sun has made its way back to our sky. It is 10:50 p.m.

At the far end of the room from the window is the narrow bed. I lie down. I sit up. I am restless. I turn off the lamp, switch off the overhead light, and walk to the window and sit in the chair, why not. With the lights off I no longer see my reflection in the window. I was sick of looking at my same old face, the only face I ever see.

Public opinion of me seems to be quite split, and if the judges' opinions are representative of what I read in the papers, they will have a difficult time agreeing on a verdict. This might take a while, but it's not like I have anywhere else to be.

There is one particular journalist who I am sure wishes that sentencing included public hanging. Michael Harrop, of London's *Evening Standard*, is the one who first called me a war criminal. He will most certainly be here to watch the trial. He called me a monster. A monster! The beasts in our imagination are far more terrifying than any beasts we could find in reality, and to this man, and his entire readership, I will never be fully human.

I expect it will never feel normal to me that I have become a public figure. The life of a scientist rarely becomes cast into the spotlight. I never anticipated this, nor all of the ways in which I have been misunderstood.

I have never met Mr. Harrop, but if I saw him on the street, I feel sure I would recognize him. His words have conjured a perfectly formed man who is about my age, looks rich and athletic, as if he knows how to play racket sports, and has a face that is handsome but smug about it. I doubt journalists get paid enough to live the kind of life I picture him having, but I can tell this is a man who comes from wealth, who was educated at the most expensive schools. (This, despite the fact that he clearly seems to have a distrust of intellectuals.) I would wager that he is the sort to match his socks to his ties, and he has galvanized a group of like-minded people to call for my death. However, his criticisms have created a backlash, too, and a collective of my fervent supporters have crystallized in opposition to him. I have noted, however, that he has carefully refrained from mentioning my religion, probably because there is no way to discuss it without polarizing the readership or politicizing his vitriol. I do give him due credit for clearly defining his hatred of me as specifically personal, rather than globally antisemitic.

When June fought to place Leora within the lap of Judaism, this is why I said no. Of course our daughter is Jewish even if we raised her secularly, but I did not want her to be publicly associated with a faith for which she could be persecuted. We didn't know where the war was going when she was born. We still don't know where it will end.

I'll tell you something that happened when Leora was still a baby, and the three of us were out together in Denver. I remember the feeling of buoyancy from being with my little family. It must have been in the spring of 1941, as Leora was just about to turn one, and the bombing of Pearl Harbor happened several months later. Even though America was not yet fighting in the war, the Americans still had their opinions. Polls were published in the papers: 83 per cent of Americans did not want the government to accept any more Jewish refugees. Officials cited the economic depression as the reason, but really, it is unfathomably difficult to defend the weaker party when it means standing up against power. People can't do it.

Anyway, we arrived at a restaurant with Leora, who was not yet walking, so she was up in June's arms. We didn't often take Leora out with us—I'm not sure how often June brought Leora out on her own, either—so this was somewhat of an occasion. June was wearing a new dress and had dressed Leora up too. I felt proud of them, proud to be with them.

The waiter commented on how adorable the baby was, et cetera. "We have a high chair in the back, would you like that?" he asked, and I was impressed. I felt so considered! I looked at June, who was distracted with Leora and didn't seem to have registered the offer. "Yes please," I said to the waiter, gently pressing my hand against June's back. What I wanted to say was *Look, darling, we belong here.* That's what I was trying to imply with my hand. *Our family belongs.* She'd been having a hard time.

The food was good, whatever it was—it was years ago, you'll forgive me for not remembering. June and I didn't have the chance to talk about much as it was an occupation to keep the baby entertained, and Leora was getting very fussy by the end of the meal.

"Oh darling, just a few more minutes"—June had hardly eaten any of her own food.

I started making funny faces to try to distract Leora, sitting opposite me, and she laughed for only a moment at each silly expression before the giggle turned to another frustrated grunt. It was then that I overheard the couple at the table behind me. Man and woman, talking amongst themselves, but clearly loud enough to be heard—wanting to be heard. I don't even want to repeat what they said. It was filled with unambiguous hatred, against me, and my wife, and our daughter—strangers to them, victims of this war. Nobody knew then, not officially at least, what was happening to the Jews in the camps—the sheer numbers of them, the complete brutality of it—but still. There were whisperings, there was a sense of what could be going on.

I looked behind me. The couple had their heads bowed to their food, but the woman, who was facing me, glanced upwards and met my eyes. We made eye contact, and she didn't flinch. I'd heard what she'd said, and she knew it. This woman's face was large but her features were very small, as if they had been swallowed by the mass of her cheeks. Her eyes were black, and if they weren't really black, I hope you'll accept the memory as symbolic.

"Did you hear that?" I whispered to June.

"Hear what?"

Leora was now fully thrashing in her high chair, trying to get her foot in the position to thrust herself up and out of her seat, and she was making headway. Her new lilac dress was covered in sauce. June squinted as Leora shrieked and knocked a cup of water down onto the floor, quite by accident, most likely. Even if June had been paying attention, the volume of our dear child would obliterate all ambient sound.

"Never mind," I said. I wouldn't make a scene in front of Leora. (Would I have made a scene otherwise? I like to think I would have.)

I looked back at the woman, who was now pretending to be deeply engaged in conversation, no longer looking at me. Her companion's back was taut, like an elastic about to snap. I'm thinking of that word, *monster*. These people were the real monsters.

Had we stayed in Europe, I've often wondered, what would have become of us?

I have been moving around this cell like a fish in a bowl. I pass the window again on my loop, pausing now to look at the sky. The ash looks surreal, like snow, but even snow, when you think about it, is absolutely surreal: *water* falls from our *sky*. I am a man who loves to fly, who loves to find answers, and yet I have no desire to explore the skies beyond this one. We live in outer space—we're already there. We are all together on this far-flung planet, landed at random in the middle of the universe, and we don't even have the answers to all *this*, yet.

There is a purity to science that is unattainable in practice. Theories are perfect, but in application, humans are involved. I have been asked whether I would agree that the tragedy of the scientist is that he is able to bring about great advances in our knowledge which mankind may then proceed to use for purposes of destruction. My answer is that this is not the tragedy of the scientist, it is the tragedy of mankind. I wonder what June would have to say about that. She brought about life, and she brought about destruction, too.

If they find me guilty tomorrow, it's only in the same way in which every human is guilty.

JUNE

My favourite memory of August is from when we were packing up to leave London, in 1936. We'd both been in dark moods and had no room in that little box of a flat, and that night, as we were trying to get organized, it was clear that neither of us wanted to touch the other, but it was very difficult not to. The paths around the bed, dresser, chair, and table accounted for about three cubic inches. I started to hum one of Mozart's Requiems so I wouldn't hear the sound of his breathing, which was driving me crazy. He got down on his knees and rummaged under the bed, I thought probably to get away from the sound of my aggressive humming, but then he emerged, still avoiding meeting my eyes, wearing my swimming cap. Swimming caps were required in order to swim in the public bathhouses in Berlin, but I had never been to a bathhouse in London, so it had been kicking around unused for months.

My rubber cap was a shade lighter than his skin, so it gave him the effect of being bald. In a flash I saw him as this bumbling, bald old man who loved me and wanted to be loved, and it broke me. I mean, it broke down my wall. He still hadn't said anything. He just kept grabbing his things and shoving them into suitcases, looking like a sad clown in a terrible half of a costume. Minutes passed. His expression never changed. Finally I stopped what I was doing, and so did he, and we looked at one another. And he laughed! He laughed in a way he so rarely ever did. Explosive and free. The rest of the time his laughter sounded like punctuation, just something to move the sentences along. And then I started laughing too, at first in a way that was kind of uncertain, and then, as he kept going, this looseness came upon me. It was sloppy, it was infectious. It was like he was giving us both this present of forgetting whatever fight or feeling had been causing the strain between us, I don't even remember what it was, and we laughed until we were delirious, and then we kept going. He looked ridiculous! I must have looked ridiculous. When I laugh that hard I snort, and that makes me snort even more, and every snort made him laugh harder in turn. It seems to me now almost like alchemy, the way August turned one thing into another. This was his gift.

That, and the way his touch could turn me into another thing, too. He was just the right height for me to feel small, enclosed within the framework of his body. He came up behind me, wrapped his hands above my pubic bone, and pressed my back against his front. My head fit underneath his chin, and he pressed down gently so that I was hugged completely. We both liked to be the one to be wooed, so it felt like a particular victory to position myself in such a way, or cast a glance, whatever it was, that gave him the spark to take over me. It was all I wanted, to be taken over.

The boat left from Southampton, a trip a couple hours south of London. Leaving our tiny apartment felt much more emotional than I'd expected. But it wasn't just about leaving our flat, or even the city, which I'd never really come to love, but our home countries, our histories. I felt so frazzled on the train to the port; I kept scanning my suitcases and bags, that feeling of forgetting something making me crazy when it all kept adding up. Two suitcases, my purse, a hat box, a bagged lunch, August's briefcase, and the large green steamer trunk. Everything was accounted for, but something was missing. I realized later: I never said goodbye to my parents.

For the two-week journey there was nothing we could do but walk the deck, look at the horizon. There was no news of home, of the outside world at all. It was awful. We were both seasick. I had thought the boat would be glamorous. I had heard stories from people who did crossings regularly. I imagined grand, wide staircases, gilt lamps, paintings in the dining room and drinking from real crystal. I at least thought that our room would have a bed large enough for us to sleep side by side, as in any hotel, and with its own bathroom too. But we were not rich, and that is not what our crossing looked like. We were refugees. We slept in bunk beds in a narrow room with no windows and used a shared toilet in the hallway. The food was worse than anything, but we were too sick to eat it anyway.

When we landed, I felt as though I'd discovered the new world. *Land*, I thought, like a lost explorer; like my daughter on the ferry. The explorers weren't sure they'd ever find land, and after a fortnight at sea, I wasn't certain about it either.

August had been offered a research position at the University of Chicago. We had been together for almost six years by this point. For months I did what felt like close to nothing, and then I got a job in Denver, Colorado. I had never been before, never heard of it to be quite honest, but mountains are in my blood. To be surrounded by impossible rocks, taller than anything I could imagine and about which I can do nothing, makes me feel at home. I didn't ask him whether I should take the job, or ask if he would come with me. We'd been living apart for so many years already, it seemed quite natural that this should continue. My position was as a professor of preventative medicine and public health at the university. I can't even say that this was my dream, because I hadn't allowed myself to dream about my own future, not really, but if that had been my reality for the rest of my life, I'd have been happy.

Not to sound too grandiose about it, but when I started working, I felt, for the first time, like people needed me. The most difficult rule, and the most important one (in my opinion), is that a doctor must find a way to treat a patient according to best practices, but also understand that each case is slightly individual. It is difficult to hold these two things in the mind: that there is a universality to each case as well as a particularity. This is where many get lost. And of course, this tension all came to a head when we were making decisions about treating our daughter.

August didn't love the mountains as much as I did. Though he did come to visit, he said he could never stay for long because the altitude made him queasy, because he had to be in his lab, because I didn't have a "comfortable chair." A comfortable chair! As though my decisions were all about his comfort; as though he and I had different requirements of ease and luxury.

When I mentioned the chair comment to my friend Katharine, who also worked at the university, she took it at face value, not reading into it all of the things that I did. She laughed, and the next day she drove over to my house and brought me a huge, green-plaid armchair she was given as a gift from her mother-in-law and kept in her basement.

"It doesn't match our decor," she said. She was generous but she was humble about it.

The chair was something to sink into. It took up half the living room and August hardly ever left it when he was there. Still, the months passed, and he made his visits brief. Eventually he avoided the chair in case I used it against him.

Katharine was in the same department as I was, but she was several years younger, just starting her career. She worked as a receptionist, a very similar position to how I had first started, but she'd been to secretarial school: this was her end-goal.

She's still there, as far as I know, while here I am—far gone, and so much further from my goals than she. If you haven't met her already then you probably never will. There'd be no reason to speak to her.

Katharine was fair. Her hair was blonde with a pink undertone to it. Strawberry, I guess they say. She had freckles all over. She must have been born with them, for they reached places the sun wouldn't: down the backs of her shoulders, her knuckles, at the nape of her neck. I never saw her without lipstick.

"He didn't like it?" she asked. I could tell she had only straightforward people in her life, people who did what they said they'd do and meant what they said, and that the struggle of my love did not appeal to her at all. She might have thought I'd envy her, for when love did come for her it would be so simple, but instead I felt a softer kind of pity. I could have had simplicity if I'd wanted it, but what I wanted was August. I wanted a love I could feel in the bottom of my heart, a love that I could never stop thinking about.

"Katharine," I said, "I don't think any chair could keep him in one place."

She felt sorry for me, and I knew there was nothing I could say to make her see that I had chosen this, that I was happy. Can you be happy but also wish things were completely different? I'm still trying to figure that out.

When August came to visit, I felt like his host. Perhaps that is what all wives feel like (though of course, I was not a wife yet). I wanted things to be nice for him. I did everything to make it feel like a holiday, even though I was still work-ing full-time. August would sit in that huge green armchair, reading the newspapers, scribbling in a notebook, or flutter-ing his eyelids in a trance that led him in and out of sleep, but his dreams were important to him. He did much work in his dreams, he said. He loved to dream, and he loved to talk about dreams, too. I once dreamed that I was a doctor in an operating room, opening up my father's heart. August said this was significant. If I dreamed about my father, he always said it represented him, August. I think that sometimes, it was actually just about my father.

My neighbours knew we weren't married. They gossiped. It was a small community and they held conservative views.

"We'd better be careful with you, June," he said as we left the house one morning to twitching curtains, "or you might lose your job because of your moral turpitude."

He was trying to be funny, but all I wanted was to be mar-ried to him.

"You'd never lose your job because of your morals, or lack thereof, would you?" We were on our way to a diner for breakfast. I knew I should never fight on an empty stomach. "A man doesn't have to worry about that."

"Ethical concerns are at the forefront of my research." He was suddenly stern, paternal.

The things August and I fought about always circled around the same thing. I needed attention. He needed free-dom. It's hard to remember the details of these fights. Just thinking about it I feel the prickle of blood in my cheeks, my heartrate quickening. First came defiance, then anger, then resentment. Resentment, if unchecked, will inevitably lead to bitterness, and that can lead to all sorts of things. But I suppose revenge isn't a feeling—it's an action.

It's almost midnight, now. The sky is the colour of a bad bruise. A lifelong insomniac, this hour of the night is familiar to me. It's not insomnia if you don't even try to sleep, though. Tonight I didn't even put on my pyjamas. I don't *want* to lose myself to dreams. I want to linger here in what is left of the period in which there is no before or after. A hotel room is already a kind of limbo. It can be anything for anyone.

I wonder what August is doing, whether he will be able to sleep. Will he have a window? Will he have a view of this strange white powder, falling like rain? It's not like rain, though, because it's light, like dandelion seeds, riding on the wind. Being in the same city as he is again, I sense his absence like a tugging.

I loved him. Of course I loved him. And he gave me my daughter, who has been my greatest love of all. Now I mourn the person I once loved, and the time we were in love together, but grief cannot be confused with love.

I am June. I'm here only as a witness. I wasn't involved in anything to do with the bomb. I don't know how to prove that to you, but you'll have more difficulty proving that I was.

II

AUGUST

My name is August. August Leo Snow. I am an American citizen. You know I've received the Atoms for Peace Award? I am innocent.

Perhaps I'm repeating myself. I'm practicing. I need to get the tone right when I introduce myself. A judge's decision is made in the postures of first impressions, and there are three of them. Three judges, three first impressions. Peter says I must be humble, but authoritative. Confident, but deferent. How to be both? Regardless of whether they consider me guilty or innocent, Peter believes that the court will perceive me as the mastermind. He says things like "the historic nature of the case" and "no precedents by which to measure it." These lines don't mean anything. All they do is set the stage; they aren't the story. The performance is what matters.

Lawyers want to win. With the truth, we just might.

"It's black and white," he said, when I told him about the patent paperwork. "We will use this in the opening statements." He shook his head and smiled, his teeth small and gappy. "I don't know why you got so worried there." Peter has nine meals a day, a five o'clock shadow by eleven in the morning, and not a care in the world.

"She's my wife," I said.

"She's not your wife anymore, old man." He patted me on the shoulder with his enormous hand and then used this as leverage to push himself up to standing.

Husband, divorcé. Humble, confident. How to be both.

Hello. *Hello.* My name is August.

I am August. August Snow.

I wasn't born a Snow. My father's name was Louis Szinow, and this is the name I was given. My brother and I changed the spelling when we left Hungary, trying to become embraced by our futures, but my sister and father kept their names, making it seem to strangers as though we were from different families. My father was livid. He said we abandoned him. He tried harder with Gabor, his favourite, but right up until his death, he never forgave me.

A black limousine picked me up from the airport to bring me to this waiting room. I consider it a waiting room and not a cell because innocent people wait in waiting rooms. It is quiet, and I am used to being alone. The driver didn't know who I was, or what I was doing here. He was polite, he was even admiring (perhaps it was my suit and hat) when he asked me where I'd come from.

"I arrived on the plane from New York," I said, and though I was quite sure that wasn't what he meant, he had no follow-up questions.

I enjoyed the views from the window in the back seat, catching glimpses of the North Sea and stretches of sand dunes, grasses as if they'd been drawn in, crosshatched. I've always appreciated the first moments in a new place, where the unfamiliar crystalizes into the known. People, paving stones, bicycles, flags, flowers. There are only so many configurations of a place. Even though it was new to me, it looked as I would have expected. The car rolled down the evening streets and, when we turned a corner, I could see that the aftermath of the accidental Bezuidenhout bombing in the spring was still evident in the gaps between buildings, buildings standing jagged like broken teeth, rubble instead of—whatever was there before. People's homes—people lived here. Some still do. With everything I saw, it felt like a goodbye.

"And how long will you be here in the Hague for?" the driver asked, looking at me in his rear-view mirror.

"Oh, I'm not quite sure yet." I crossed my hands in my lap. "We'll see how things go."

"I see," he smiled. "So, is it business or pleasure?"

"I'll be seeing my ex-wife for the first time in years," I said, which was the truth, or the hope, at least, but not the answer.

"Ah, so you're here for *love*," he beamed. This was a reason he could understand, and he chose to paint his whole impression of me with this information alone. "You want to win her back, don't you?"

I smiled, my thoughts turning to June. This was likely the last encounter I would have with a stranger who did not know who I was, I thought, and what I have done. After tomorrow, regardless of my plea, I will have no such privacy. "She was the love of my life," I said. "I asked her to meet me here."

He'll see me on the news tomorrow and tell everyone, with horror and pride in his voice: *I drove that criminal in my car! Can you believe it?*

I say "criminal," but Peter advises that I maintain neutrality. I am August.

When I think of June, I see her laughing, always laughing. She had dark, wavy hair—I always said "fuzzy," and that always made her angry—cropped into a soft sphere around her head. Elegant to the point of austerity, and yet somehow equally warm. A private kind of warmth, a warmth that was only for me. I often think that when we truly love someone, knowing them so intimately as to complicate everything, nothing about them can exist in just one bubble. We pile on descriptions to get more and more specific, to make them less and less like anyone else. Not contradictions, exactly—more like qualifications. We do this in science too, of course. Narrow the field in order to intensify the truth. June was joyful and prone to melancholy; she was tender but always maintained a distance.

One time, after over a year of being together, June was telling a story at a friend's dinner party. A story I had never heard before. "Honey," I remember saying, "I haven't heard that one!" I was more than surprised; I thought we had shared everything already. I was—hurt. Hurt that something about June could be outside of my awareness. That others could know things about her that I did not. She thought this silly, of course, but didn't take it as seriously as she might have. As, perhaps, she should have. This occasion opened up to me the capacity of my possessiveness, which I tried to deal with and repress, but it also alerted me to the depths of my need for her.

"We don't need July," June said, less than a week after we'd met. "Just June and August."

I am hungry but I cannot eat. I sometimes wonder about the other things I might be feeling. The only feelings I am used to listening to these days are the immediate ones. Hunger, tiredness, discomfort. These are more easily quantifiable. I miss June, and I miss my daughter, but my longing is physical. It is pain.

Despite all of this, I am happy. My happiness exists apart from the tarnishing of the physical world. I pace the fifteen steps between this window and the bed, sensing the hunger grow in the belly of my heart, and as I think of how little my love matters to my daughter or my wife, I carry proudly my defiant happiness. The years will trundle on, children will yawn over the history books detailing this trial, and no matter what happens tomorrow, all of this will pass, and my happiness will remain, for I have been lucky. I am one of the lucky ones to have found love.

JUNE

In our total of twelve years together, we went on one vacation: up to Canada, through the Rocky Mountains. It was 1938, and I'd been living in Denver for about a year. He planned other trips for us. Bermuda, Hollywood, back to Europe. But we never went.

August mapped the route from Denver to Vancouver and rented a fancy-looking red car. He figured it would take about thirty hours to do the whole journey, which he planned to pace out over five days and four nights. I don't like to drive, and August was terrible at it. We'd travelled together so often, but never for pleasure. I didn't really know what to expect. I brought my nicest clothes, thought of where I might be when I wore each outfit. When I pictured us there—wherever, at a restaurant, or by the beach, or walking down an unfamiliar street arm in arm, whatever we might do as a Couple On Vacation—I pictured us as the couple who didn't fight.

That first day we headed off after breakfast and were planning to arrive in Salt Lake City by dinnertime. We were both tense and irritable, all of our basic needs piling up at the end of the day, and I was desperately looking forward to arriving at the hotel. August loved hotels. There was a reason he chose to spend much of his time living in them. Hotels allowed him to live comfortably without having to do anything so terrestrial as washing his own linens.

I kept the window rolled down, though August kept insisting I roll it back up as it was noisy and "slowed us down," he said, which sounded like crap to me. It was too hot, though, and while the car was a fancy one it wasn't fancy enough to have a radio, and the only thing I could do to pass the time was hold my arm out into the air as it whipped past, shifting the shape and position of my fingers to move my whole arm up and down over the air, as though my hand were a sail and my body was the boat.

All roads essentially look the same, anywhere you are. We could have been anywhere I've ever been, or anywhere I've not. Grey asphalt, grassy shoulders, clouds in the sky. Here, though, there was a particular rusty look about the land, as if nobody had taken care of it. The rocks were ruddy, the fields parched. I'd packed some snacks but hadn't eaten anything other than an apple since breakfast. I fantasized about what we'd have for dinner. The hotel was an expensive one. To start, I wanted a shaken cocktail in a frosty glass, something sour and bitter.

I was holding the map, but my eyes were closed. I was trying to enjoy the moment. The sun was right before us, bright and low on the horizon. I knew we'd be there soon—road signs started saying Utah. August surely didn't need me to navigate anymore.

I hadn't realized I was sleeping until I woke up when the car stopped moving. August parked the car and came around to open my door. He picked me up and gave me a deep, serious kiss. "I will fuck you as soon as we find a bed," he said, changing the mood immediately, erasing the tension of the drive. I would have made a bed of myself in the parking lot if I could.

My body was warm and I was happy. There was a very grand church next to the hotel, tiny windows like paper cuts in the pale stone, and turrets on the tops of the many towers. Christians could show off all they wanted; they had nothing to be afraid of.

August and I walked in through one of the revolving doors, past the doormen and valets. I smiled, thanking them for nothing, for letting me be there. I sat on one of many plush benches in the enormous, vaulted foyer, warmly lit, glowing with the feeling of smug satisfaction that luxury bestows, as though we all simply deserved this. There were so many new people to look at, their faces all weird and different, their lives secret from mine. In Denver, I felt like I'd seen everyone already.

August's broad back filled out his tan linen jacket so nicely. I watched from my bench as he addressed the man behind the check-in desk, who was very tiny and fair. I tried to scan the lobby for the bar, wondering if I could go ahead and place my order.

This was taking longer than I expected. The man's eyes were too close together and the lids were pronounced, like awnings, and his eyebrows had a feminine arch. There was this foolish hat that was part of his uniform, a little round thing he must have had to pin into place. To be honest, I didn't even register this man until I noticed the volume rise. That's when I stood up to see what was going on. Until then, this man had been insignificant to me, just a small step in the process.

"I'm sorry, sir," the man said, not looking August in the eye.

I could feel the heat from August's body as I stood close. "I've already *paid*," he said sternly, as though that were the issue.

"We will refund your account, of course."

"August? What's happening?" I whispered, but not privately. That man would surely have heard me. "Are they overbooked?"

There was a heavy pause as August, hands shaking, stared at this man, and I wondered whether something big was about to happen—if he'd lunge, hit, spit, scream—but after the moment had passed, the air still thick, August put his hand behind my back and grabbed our suitcase.

"What is it?" I asked again, so naïve.

The man behind the desk did not look at me, and did not respond.

"No Jews," August said, as he guided me back to the entrance firmly.

At first I didn't understand what he'd said, since it was delivered with absolutely no tone or emotion. He could have said anything. Within moments, though, I felt the warmth of my body drain out as immediately as if a plug had been pulled, leaving me naked in a cold, empty bathtub.

The walk back through the lobby had none of the same feelings as the walk in. To be unwelcome changes how everything looks. The soft luxury of it all was now cold and sharp.

August and I said nothing as we walked back to the car, put the suitcase in the trunk, and eased back onto the road. I could tell he felt ashamed, whereas I felt angry, but both of us were voiceless.

We drove for a while, watching the sky lose its colour, and then August pulled into the parking lot of a comparatively dismal motel. The couple behind the desk gave us a room for cheap without hesitation. The blankets on the two twin beds were well-worn.

I had a bath, August read, and when I came out, wrapped in a towel, he pulled the curtains.

"Are you hungry?" I asked. "I'm starving."

He shook his head and put down whatever newspaper he'd found in the room. He came towards me, turned me around, and took off my towel. He fucked me like I was a problem to solve. I gave him that. From my angle, his face looked shadowy and enormous, ancient and sad. If he was old then I must be getting older, too. I wondered what his parents looked like, which of them he might resemble. It's strange to love someone in isolation from their past, with no context for what came before you met them. Children assume their parents didn't exist before the child themselves were born, and this felt sort of similar. August existed only for me.

We slept in our separate beds that night without having any dinner at all. I just wanted to go home.

—

"Have you ever wanted children?" I asked him over toast the next morning.

"I've never had the opportunity for them," he responded.

"It's not usually something that just *comes up*, August. Did you want kids when you were little?"

"I didn't think about it."

"I used to nanny a little girl, have I told you about that?"

He shook his head, mouth full, and wiped jam from his lips.

I couldn't believe that I wouldn't have told him about Trude, as she had meant so much to me, but I can see now that so much of my being with August had been keeping myself open to him, bending towards him in this way that erased my own self, so perhaps it's true that it simply had not come up. "Well, she was the daughter of my father's friend, and I lived with their family for a summer when I was eighteen, before moving to Berlin. She was so sweet, she was around three or four, and there was this—I don't know, animalistic sense to her, to the way she loved me. I don't think I'd thought about having children before that."

August often told me stories about his younger sister and brother, how he was the captain of the ship when they played together. I could tell he had loved being a big brother, and when I saw him interact with children it was clear that he loved them, but I could never get him to talk about whether he wanted children of his own. I had never asked him directly, so I did: "What do you think about it now? Do you want children *now*?"

"Right now?" he put down his knife and fork, "I want you."
He said it in a way that felt kind, even a little dismissive, rather
than passionate.

Eventually, August and I decided to wed. Or, more accurately,
he finally agreed to my demands. I should have anticipated
that this technicality wouldn't solve any of our problems. He
loved the world in general rather than loving me, or anyone,
in particular.

The engagement changed nothing, of course. He delayed in
setting the date, evading my questioning. I finally pinned him
down to a quick affair at the city hall in New York, timed for
when I would be out East anyway for a conference. I bought a
simple yellow silk dress that fell below my knees and had
a matching jacket. Little daisies were embroidered along the
edges in a matching thread and I fidgeted my fingers along
the edges of the petals, feeling the subtle ridges. Katharine
helped me pick out some satin shoes that I got dyed to match.
At twenty-eight, I was the only one of my friends still unwed.
I had my hair done to copy a picture from a magazine and felt
more beautiful than I'd ever felt before, even though none of
this was how I had pictured my wedding as a child.

We didn't invite our families, but I did write to my parents
to tell them. They'd never even met August. They might have,
had he visited long enough when I was in Vienna for medical
school, but beyond that, it was impossible for them to keep up
with our nomadic life. The journey to America would have
been too expensive.

They sent money as a gift, and my mother also sent me her pearl necklace I'd always admired as a little girl. The clasp was a fine gold oval with tiny pearls embedded in the shape of a simple flower that looked just like the daisies on my dress. I wore that on my wedding day too. I keep it in a box, now. My mother's note said simply: *Go with love.*

This is the last note I have from her. I sent a thank-you letter, in which I told her all about the wedding, but this letter was among those that were eventually returned.

August and I were in the waiting room together while another ceremony was being completed. It was just the two of us—we planned to use a city witness. This was not what I had wanted, not at all, but an almost-invisible wedding was the only way August would agree to the plan. Our appointment was at 3 p.m. At 2:45, August was pacing back and forth, complaining of the wait, saying the room really should be ready for us already if we were going to begin on time.

I rolled my eyes and held my hands as I sat in one of the waiting room chairs.

At 3 p.m., he said he had other things he could be doing.

"August," I said, with more sympathy than I should have given him. "Surely you don't have any other appointments on our wedding day?"

There were no windows in the waiting room; it was really more of a corridor. I know he would have been happier if he could have seen outside. I'd come to visit the hall previously, and the room itself was lovely, south-facing with big windows overlooking the skyline. That was the reason I'd chosen it.

"If this place had windows," August said, seemingly reading my mind, "I would throw myself out of them."

"*August.*" I treated him as a petulant child, not as my petulant near-husband, which was my mistake. I didn't want to marry him any less, I just wanted to get it over with.

At 3:15, when the couple who'd been in the room marched proudly out, holding hands, their friends and family showering them with rice confetti, he decried the disorganization of America's bureaucracy. I hoped this group was too happy to pay attention to him.

A few minutes later, a clerk came to the door to inform us that it was our turn.

"Do I look nice?" I asked August, really hoping he'd say yes.

"You always look nice," he said, and he took my hand.

The ceremony was forgettable and there are no photographs.

After the wedding and a weekend in a hotel, our "honeymoon," I flew back to Denver and August went back to Chicago. There was still no plan to live together. I was a married woman living a single life, and this is exactly what he wanted. Trapped at arm's length. I felt like such a fool.

We didn't make an official home together ("together") until we'd been married for a year, and only then because the lease was coming up on my small apartment. I wanted more space, and naturally I wanted to share my space with August. It took a long time to settle on where we would live. His work was in Chicago and, while he didn't have to be in an office every day, the technologies in his lab there did not exist anywhere else in the world. My work was at a hospital in Denver—and if I wasn't there every day, I would not be able to continue to say I worked there. I won. That didn't mean he moved to Denver permanently, just that it was in our home there that he would hang some extra suits and keep a toothbrush as well as some of his files, if only for him to have something to work on during the longer stays. (I always hoped he would have longer stays.) In Chicago, he kept a small apartment, and in New York, his room at the hotel was always made available at even a moment's notice if a meeting arose. I never asked what kinds of meetings he took there.

The new house was close enough to the hospital that I could walk, but our neighbourhood, like most suburban neighbourhoods, was not designed for walking. Many of the streets didn't even have sidewalks. The front gardens were all so beautiful, though, and how was one to enjoy them driving by at thirty miles an hour in a low-slung car with windows too high to peer over? I hated driving. I refused to get my license. If I ever needed a car, I called for a driver. I wanted to walk, to be propelled by the power of my own body. Cars burn so much fuel, too. August was determined to find a way for them to run on nuclear energy, like everything else he was planning, but that's not where the money was. The money wanted things to stay exactly as they were.

So I walked, lingering at every garden, appreciating them as I had once appreciated paintings, which were much more plentiful than front gardens where I came from. I came to understand that the way a garden is designed mimics the way a composer creates an opera—it's long-duration art, meant to come alive in stages. In the winter, the hellebore that rewards you if you work hard enough to notice it, blending in with the greenery; at the first sign of spring come the royal-purple crocuses, their flamboyant yellow hearts emerging shortly after; then later the lupins arrive, first meekly, then growing into pastel flame-throwers; then the lilac arrives like hand-sculpted ornaments and smelling of candy; and as summer barrelled onwards I'd get to see the drunk hydrangeas toppling effervescently from their stalks, and the spiky crowned purple coneflowers, beloved by the bees. I taught myself the names of all of the plants, all of the trees too, because knowing their names made it so that I could greet them as friends. *Hello, narrowleaf cottonwood. Good morning, ponderosa pine.* My little community.

But even though I loved the gardens beyond measure, their beauty made me feel angry, and embarrassed. My own gardens, both front and back, were nothing. Rubble and tufts of overgrown, bleached-out grass. These beautiful gardens mocked me, but I could not get enough of them. I found myself spending more time on walks than I did at home, hungry to be in the presence of this beauty. I was under the delusion then that I could only enjoy something if it belonged to me. I still feel that way.

AUGUST

Growing up in Pest, I'd never heard of so many of the places June and I went—Denver, Vancouver—and yet here was a whole world that had also never heard of me. On our trip to British Columbia, we went swimming in the Pacific on a mild, windless day, yet even the tiny waves were monumental to me, and the water was the colour of ice. June ran down at top speed, crashing right into the ocean in her red bathing suit with her arms wide open, and I stayed paddling in the shallows, tentatively letting the incoming tide tongue at my feet on the pebbled beach. I envied her freedom, her bravery. She was too focused on what she was doing to be aware that I was watching. It didn't feel like a performance. She was so wholly absorbed in the pleasure and motion, the cold of the water, the rocks underfoot. Like a child. And then she turned back.

"What would happen if you came in?" she called to me, the sun behind her, leaving her face in shadows but for the bright white of her smile that created its own light.

I was forty years old and I didn't know how to swim, but I couldn't tell her that; I'd never told her. "I'd melt," is what I said.

She ran forward and splashed the water towards me, but I was too far for it to reach me. "Then melt with me!"

I clenched the muscles in my legs, making myself as tall and straight and solid as I could. And then, you know what? I ran.

"Yes!" she cried.

I didn't stop. I ran right past her until the water was above my nipples and I couldn't run anymore. The water was frigid and it made me forget what I'd been worrying about. I gasped. I felt the smooth rocks under my feet. I let the cold take my body until I was part of the sea itself.

I loved her so much.

I use the past tense because love is nothing but the accumulation of shared time, and the more time that passes apart from one another, the less it exists.

I miss them more than I thought possible.

There's still enough time—we have a long night ahead of us—so let me tell you about another memory, one of my earliest. By the time I was twelve years old, in 1910, my family had moved from our apartment in Pest to a beautiful art nouveau villa in the Garden District, where decorous mansions squatted far back from the road. The fact that we could afford such a home in such a neighbourhood meant my father's engineering business had obviously grown, though I wasn't much thinking about that. My parents didn't talk about money with us and so I had the privilege of not thinking about it. As the city continued to grow after unification, there were many bridges to be built.

For my birthday that year, my parents allowed me to take my brother for a walk to the zoo, which wasn't far from our new house. My brother was my only friend, really. As I mentioned, I didn't take to people well. We didn't have to share a room but we chose to, meaning we could read my favourite H. G. Wells books together instead of sleeping and use what had been my brother's bedroom as our playroom, laboratory, office. I taught him how to build a radio and together we wrote a story about a little boy who discovered fire. We taught ourselves how to bind it and we read it to our family after dinner. I digress. Going to the zoo for my birthday was the first time I was allowed out without either my mother or father or a governess. I wore a navy-blue V-neck sweater under my jacket, and my best brown felt cap—flat-brimmed, flat-topped, not one of the children's cloth caps I usually wore, and which Gabor wore then. It wasn't such an occasion for him. He was still a young boy; I was the grown-up now, and I had the hat to show for it. Holding Gabor's hand, I turned right onto the Fasor, a broad boulevard connecting the central shopping district of Budapest to City Park, our destination. With my other hand I held a closed umbrella, just in case, and I swung it in a way that I imagined would look gentlemanly as we passed under the rows of flowering horse-chestnut trees. I can see now how incongruous, how ridiculous, I must have looked—fancying myself a twelve-year old gentleman.

We walked through the park, past the metro entrance, and beyond the Gallery of Fine Arts. My brother was chattering away like a wind-up toy, pointing out everything that caught his eye. Through a grand archway, held up by the backs of four stone elephants, was the entrance to the zoo. I bought the tickets with the money my father had given me and which I'd been feeling for in the breast pocket of my jacket every few moments along the way. Once inside, Gabor said he wanted to go straight to the elephants. They lived within a brick structure that was shaped somewhat like a synagogue. I looked up when I sensed the wind change, and saw the clouds were quickening. I was right to bring my umbrella.

Six or seven of the elephants were out in the open yard, but there was a moat between us and them. The children on our side of the moat had peanuts in paper bags and the elephants were reaching their trunks across the water to try to sniff up the treats. The rain began to fall, and I noticed my favourite elephant emerge from the structure. He was the real object of our journey: he was the largest and oldest of all the elephants and I adored him. So did Gabor. I wished I could touch his skin. I longed to know whether it felt like my father's leather satchel, or a leaf of paper, or my grandmother's feet, with their thick, dry skin. Those were the three choices I had whittled it down to from dozens, after weeks of thinking. I had reason enough to believe that I would never get to touch the elephant, though. I stepped up onto the ledge and gripped the railing, my hands next to my brother's.

"How old do you think he is?" Gabor asked.

"We can ask one of the zookeepers," I said. "I wouldn't want to guess at random."

The rain was getting heavier. The crowds were thinning, but I saw no zookeeper. I fiddled with the strap of the umbrella and, as I leaned over, my brown hat was caught by the wind and skimmed right into the moat.

"Shoot," I said, trying to get footing in between the metal railings so as to reach a little further. I flipped the umbrella around and used the handle as a hook to try to fish out the hat. My feet kept slipping, but this time I got it. Just as soon as I'd lifted my hat out of the water, though, the elephant—my elephant— nosed his trunk through his side of the fence and aimed right for my hat. The tip of an elephant's trunk looks like an open mouth, and seeing one for the first time up close, I was fascinated to see its wobbly lips gumming for the rim of my beautiful cap.

"Hey!" I called, believing the elephant would understand if I explained.

I tugged, but the elephant tugged harder. It was an uneven match: my ninety pounds to his thirteen thousand. Slowly, slowly, the elephant stepped back, his four cylindrical, cement-coloured legs evenly pacing the earth, dust blooming with every raindrop. He yanked me back with him. My chest was pressed against the railing and I was beginning to realize how much it was hurting me. If I kept at it I was going to lose my umbrella, or my arm, perhaps even my life. I let go.

(In the passing graze I got of the skin of the elephant's trunk, I did notice that it felt like the third option: my grandmother's feet.)

Proudly, the elephant waved his prize in the air, as if showing off to the others—his friends, his family, I don't know.

Do you know what the elephant did next? He brought his gummy-lipped trunk to his giant mouth, stuffed my hat into the hole, and chewed. I stared, livid, defeated, humiliated.

"Let's go," I said, grabbing Gabor's hand, not bothering anymore to put up the umbrella. We were already wet. We would get wetter. "It won't come out the other end of the beast before tomorrow. We'll come back then." I pulled Gabor, who kept turning around, trying to get a glimpse of the scene we were leaving behind, but I just walked onward.

The walk home felt shorter than the way there, as it always does.

In 1941, when Leora was several months old, June received a bundle of all of the letters she'd sent to her parents. Returned to sender, no explanation, wrapped in twine. She pushed them across the table to me when I got home for dinner one evening.

"Oh," I said. I picked them up, turned the package over, looking for some note, or clue. "What do you think—?"

June shrugged. "They don't even know about her." She nodded her head in the direction of where Leora was laying on a blanket, blissfully gnawing on clothespins. June seemed detached. She didn't look me in the eye. I reached my hand across the table but she didn't reach back. I wonder what she felt.

Oh, how I wish I'd asked.

I wish I had asked her to tell me about her parents. Then, or before. If she had talked about it, maybe it would have helped her to pull the memories out of her heart, out of the deepest coils of her brain, and put them into the sunlight of consciousness. I don't even know their names. We wouldn't find out what had happened, for certain, for several years. We had no idea. That kind of thing, it's not something you can imagine. If I had known, I could have behaved differently. No. I didn't know, and I still could have been better.

Oh, how I regret not making myself into a little boat, as my mother had said, and trying to reach the island of my wife.

It's past midnight now, and I thought that tiredness would kick in eventually, but there is an energy keeping me alert tonight. I touch the window with my palm, mostly just for something to touch. In the years since I've seen my daughter I've often wondered how I would speak to her, and how she would speak to me. Now that she's five, almost six, we could converse in a way that we couldn't the last time I saw her. She will have her own interests, her own opinions. I wonder whether she is grateful for me, for what I did for her, or whether her mother has convinced her otherwise. Or perhaps Leora doesn't even think about me at all. This would be worse.

JUNE

The pregnancy was unplanned. I don't like the word "accident." I was twenty-nine—most women my age were already mothers. But I had just started to get comfortable in Denver, to feel valued in my position, to know my patients, and my community. I was, for the first time in a while, happy. When I found out, I knew I would have to leave my career, and—oh, I feel that awful mother-shame admitting this—that little seedling of regret was my first reaction to the news.

It was August, actually, who convinced me to go into medicine. He has this ability where, like a telescope magnifying only the best parts, he allows people see themselves the way that he sees them. He is able to seduce people, make them feel whatever he wants them to feel. It starts off charming—I fell in love with him, after all—but now I see it differently.

"I know you're interested in epidemiology," he said, over a dinner I'd cooked at his apartment one night.

"I think so, yes." It felt embarrassing, somehow, to have him talk to me like this. I was touched that he was thinking of me, but it was difficult for me to imagine the future—especially a future that could mean leaving Berlin, and leaving him.

"Have you thought about pursuing a degree in medicine?"

"To become a doctor?"

"Don't you think that would be a good fit?"

It could have been different. I really believe that. We could have approached things differently, as we had done with our relationship up until that point. Nobody would have ever described us as conventional. But he stopped seeing me as a scientist, as an equal, when I became pregnant. I could feel my loss of ranking in the way everyone else looked at me, but it was the way that he spoke to me that made me lose respect for myself. As though it was a given that I would surrender my past self and transform wholly into *mother*. I wanted to be a mother; I don't want you to pity me or think me ungrateful, but I also wanted to retain some sense of my *self*.

August was also the one who turned me away from medicine when he didn't defend me, or encourage me, or help me find a way to keep my job.

I received the news at a doctor's appointment I had made to investigate the source of my persistent nausea. I wrote to August in Chicago to tell him the news. It didn't feel urgent, no need for a phone call. There were eight more months of waiting, after all.

I can't remember how it came up, whether he asked me to do it directly or merely assumed I would, but throughout the course of our relationship, and with an increased intensity during my pregnancy, as though he could sense my role was shifting, August depended on me to cut out newspaper clippings and manage his paperwork. The few files here and there gradually became a highly organized archive. He took my expertise seriously in that he would ask for my medical opinion in order to confirm his own beliefs about his health, but he took his career seriously in that he thought he needed an archivist.

August was a compulsive patent-filer, and part of managing his paperwork often included organizing this material, which dated back years. There was that icebox with Einstein, and then it was vapour lamps, and electron microscopes, and cyclotrons. There were patents on small components of larger things, and on minor updates to existent systems, and on entirely new ideas, which popped up for him as naturally as flowers in spring. I don't remember them all. Filing patents, I quickly learned, takes months of administration and waiting and often yields nothing.

We had enough money, but he was greatly preoccupied by his *future* earnings. This is what all of his patents were for. Retirement, savings, to build a wall around him. Money was a constant obsession for him. He had "high operating costs."

That's how he put it. His concern was contagious: it infected me, too.

We saw each other several more times throughout my pregnancy. He got to watch our baby grow inside of me, he got to feel her kicks. For the most part he was present and loving and imaginative with this baby behind my belly, talking to the moon in me, writing letters to our future child. But with me, August was tempestuous, and not without misgivings. He'd ask how my work was going—meaning his archives, and not my job.

"We never discussed this," he said once, when I was telling him how I wished he could be with me more often, and help prepare our home for the baby. "I never asked to be a father."

He was in Chicago when she came, three weeks early. Her birth was the closest to death I've ever felt. The pain swallowed me. I could see the end of it all. My obstetrician was on vacation when I went into labour and I knew none of the medical team on call. I was completely alone and I missed my mother with this intense animal instinct, in a way I never had previously, despite all of the time and distance between us. I wanted my parents to be there with me, to be the first to meet their grandchild, to tell me she looked just like me, to tell me she was beautiful.

I don't know if you know this already from your research, but my family was killed at the concentration camp in Buchenwald in 1938, about two years before Leora was born. I hadn't even known they'd been taken. We'd lost touch. *I* lost touch.

My new life swept me away. For years, I didn't know. You can read about it. That's not what we're here to talk about.

It seemed I had been in the hospital bed, roiling in agony, screaming and naked, for all of my life. There was no time. The lights were too bright so I kept my eyes closed. I was entirely alone. A nurse came up closer to my head—everyone had been below my waist, focused on what was going on down there—and asked if I wanted some ice chips. The two words didn't make sense in combination to me. *Ice. Chips.* Chips? The nurse was standing right in front of a light and so her short, yellowish-greyish hair was haloed while her face was cast into a dark shadow. I tried to find her eyes. To find them, I had to shift my perspective, adjust my eyes to the dark, and when they clicked into place I had a sense of such sudden clarity. Someone was there. Someone was here. Her eyes were within radiant beams of wrinkles, and this sign of her age made me feel trusting towards her. She was old, she had seen this before, she knew what she was doing. I felt brave enough to articulate to her my biggest fear: "Am I going to die?"

She laughed, and the beams around her eyes got deeper, somehow brighter. She held my hand. I wondered if she was an angel. I wondered if she was my mother. "Darling girl," she said, "you will die, but not from this."

And then a deep heaviness pushed through me, the pain was something beyond pain, but I knew I would not die from this so I let it open me right up. I let it break me. I roared, like a predator, not from the pain, but from—I don't know. The transformation?

A voice spoke in an authoritative tone—"4:07 a.m., time of birth." So time had in fact still been happening, and it had been hours, not lifetimes that I had been in my state of suspension between worlds; there were people, at least six of them, all around me; and the baby was on the outside of my body. At 4:07 a.m. on the sixth of June, 1940, I got to meet my baby for the first time. She was handed to me in a white flannel blanket by one of the people in the room.

"It's a girl," the person said. I don't know anything more about this person other than that they had hands with which they passed me my baby.

A girl. My girl. Leora.

"Hello, Leora," I said. And again, as with the pain, the people disappeared from my vision. Perhaps they left the room, their job complete. All I saw was this new tiny human. This perfect thing. Her arms and legs stretched out, for the first time free from the constraints of the womb, but, like little springs, they contracted right away, not yet ready to explore the full extent of their reach. I held my baby tentatively, but she didn't know. She didn't know I was her mother, what it was to be held, what it was to breathe air. This was all new to her. Her eyelids were sealed closed and she was so quiet it was a little eerie. I thought babies screamed, but from the beginning, she was a quiet one. She listened. After the examinations of both baby and me were complete, and my bleeding was under control, I was sent home. She was nine hours old, and we went home together.

The house was ready for a baby in an objective sense, but I hadn't known what a baby would be like. What *this* baby would be like. All of her blankets and clothes were neatly folded and placed, in such a beautiful, orderly fashion, into the chest of drawers I'd bought and painted butter-yellow for her in the days I had been waiting for her arrival. But it was summer, and it was hot, and so she never wore any clothes. It didn't seem worth it to put them on only to take them off. She wore diapers and I wrapped her in gauzy blankets and I held her, I didn't let go.

The house was so quiet, it didn't feel right. She made her noises, but I was hushed into a reverence that I see now was the understudy of fear. Afraid of waking her, afraid of startling her, afraid of missing a moment that she might need something. The days became different things, units of time parcelled in completely new ways. She was one day old when her eyes opened, then three days old, and five days old, but in those five days she had only been awake for, maybe, six hours. And I, on the other hand, had probably only slept for a total of six hours in that time. That shouldn't count as five days, not for either of us. In the blur of minutes, of asynchronous wakefulness, I experienced constant explosions of peace. Everything else fell away. But the peace hinged on a precipice of some kind, as if I were above the eye of a hurricane. All I had to do was hold her, and as I held her, my thoughts reticulated from the love of this tiny perfect creature outward to this too-big realization of a sort of web of love that connected the whole world. My love felt both philosophical and so of-this-world it was almost . . . banal, yet it felt so revolutionary to me. And on the flip side of all of this love was the knowledge that it could not last forever, and this opened up the greatest tragedy I had ever known. I had known for as long as I could remember that I would die—this isn't a fact that had previously caused me any existential angst—but knowing that I would not be alive for every second of my baby's life was impossible. I could not get over it. Any time I felt one of the many daily surges of delight upon seeing my baby I started to become sick with anxiety. In those early days, I was so worried about an accident befalling me or illness ravaging me that I hadn't even considered that *she* could be the one to fall down the abyss. That I could miss her, not get to see her grow up, because *she* would be gone.

We came up with the name together, August and I. We decided it would be Leo for a boy, after the nickname his father had given him, which also worked for a girl, Leora; so before she was born, we called my belly "Little Leo." I didn't picture a lion, I pictured the stars.

I had always liked more classic names, like Mary, or Elizabeth. But I wanted him to feel involved, and connected, so I let him leave his imprint on our child. (I suppose we didn't exactly come up with the name together, then, but the idea to let him have it was mine.) The baby's connection to me would be a given: as the mother, my rights were inalienable, instantaneous. Maybe it's also true that I wanted to bond August to us in a more permanent way. A man can walk away from a woman and child with no trace, no consequences; but I thought, and I didn't say this to him or anyone else, that if he felt closer to our baby, then he would be less likely to leave me.

Once in a while, when it became necessary to leave the house, I would bring a blanket out to the park down the street and find a tree for us to sit under, let her lie in the shade and watch the sun passing through the leaves, feel the shadows playing on her body. The warmth of the sun beamed directly onto her magnolia-pink belly. What was she thinking? Was she capable of thought? Can thoughts exist without language? It seemed to me that Leora lived in a world of sensation. She lived only in the present. This had its advantages and disadvantages. The main disadvantage was that I could not convince her, if she was hungry or cold or wet, that there would ever be a time when she would not feel this way. She screamed, inconsolable, and I could not rationalize with her. That kind of life seemed terrifying to me—to know nothing, to understand nothing, to have no control—and I admired her so much for not being afraid. She approached it all with curiosity, and pleasure, and full-throated rage.

But in that moment, on the blanket in the park, and all the others just like it, she accepted all the details of the present as a gift.

The baby didn't feel quite real to me in those first few weeks. I still wonder, if August had been there with me, whether it would have all felt more tangible. In my intense solitude—in the role of carer, though I had a constant companion, I felt more profoundly alone—I started to feel the borders between things becoming finer, less distinct. Wakefulness, sleep. Hunger, satiation. Joy, terror. Life and death. My fear of dying intensified, yes, but I also became afraid that since I had done nothing to deserve my baby, someone might decide that I didn't deserve to keep her.

I fed her. Changed her. Picked her up, lay her down. Burped her. Washed her, washed the clothes, the linens, the diapers, myself. It was a choreography I performed with no rehearsals and no audience every two hours round the clock. It felt as if I had moved to a part of the world where I knew nobody and did not speak the language and was not allowed to bring anything from my past life. Actually, I had already done that. This was worse.

If August had been there, he might have been able to puncture the solipsism of my depression. It doesn't feel right to call it that, for I was also ecstatic, but this was how the doctors diagnosed me retroactively. If it comes to this in the trial, I can lean on my documented medical history as an explanation for my impulsive behaviour.

My days with Leora were so quiet, so intense, but also unwatched, entirely undocumented. This invisibility was precious to me, as I've said, but it also made me feel isolated. If there was no witness, how could I prove it was happening?

The friend inside my head became inaccessible to me during this time. I didn't know what to tell her to make her feel better. I couldn't think of any script for her; I couldn't think of anything anyone could say that would make me feel less alone.

Every day I checked my only house plant for dead leaves and relished finding any, plucking the shriveled brown ones from their healthy green family. It was called a prayer plant.

I don't know why. The leaves rose in the evening and settled back down when the sunlight returned. I watched this happen like it was the only thing I wanted to do in the world. I guess this is a form of prayer.

I thought about getting a goldfish for something different to look at.

I wrote to August, hoping this would provide something, some kind of documentation. I wanted to be the narrator of this life, not just its only witness. I wrote so there would be evidence.

Dear August,

I spend a lot of time wondering what you looked like as a baby. I wish I could have met you then. Having Leora here makes me feel closer to you as you are now, but also to your infant self. I wonder what she inherited from you, and what comes from me, and what comes from her many ancestors whom she will never meet.

Today Leora is five weeks old. I stare at her body but can't quite see it as a whole thing. I see it in parts. The taut, flat part of skin where cheekbone turns to temple, above the curved peach of her cheek. The delicate wisps of her eyebrows. How could I have grown eyebrows inside of my body? When I stroke her back, the skin ripples like sand being blown by the wind. But I think I also have a hard time seeing her as a whole baby, not just parts of a baby, because the entirety of her existence feels mystical, even though I know the science of it. Even if I didn't, it's common sense.

I know babies. I've seen babies. But I didn't know my body could make one.

She is beautiful. She is so beautiful I can't quite believe it. This is the happiest I've ever felt, I think, and that carries with it this deep grief, for I know that it will end. Our present selves exist only in this moment and when it is over, these selves will be gone, with nobody to remember them.

I know your work is there, but your family is here. I wish you would come. I don't feel like myself. I would be happy if motherhood had made me become a new person, I suppose that would have been fine, but for now I feel like no person.

I didn't send the letter.

And then, she woke up. She woke up! After three or four months it was like her brain turned on and all she wanted to do was learn what it was to be alive in this world. She became real. I mean, she had always been real, but she became real to *me*. Not just the shape of a baby, but *my baby*. She smiled. Her first smile. It came from nowhere. I didn't have to do anything to elicit the smile, there was just some happiness within her that she wanted to express. I started to wonder if maybe there were smiles I missed, whether she grinned while I was sleeping or washing dishes, and I felt, I'm a little embarrassed to admit this, jealous. Of what? Of whatever — the air, I suppose? — that got to witness her happiness. Or maybe jealous of her, of my daughter's mind, capable of generating her own joy. But her smiles made me smile, it was impossible not to, and I became addicted to making more of them. My baby. I could keep her alive with my body, and she could keep us happy with whatever it was that sparked through her.

Her toes! Her toes. This will sound vain, or selfish, or something, but my daughter felt more familiar to me, and this familiarity in turn allowed me to love her more, when I saw that her toes were miniature versions of my own. The same narrowness, the same-shaped nailbeds, the way the second toe is positioned at an angle to the first; the way the knuckle on the fourth is slightly closer to the top than the proportions on the rest. I could picture my mother holding my toes, feeling this same mystery, and awe, and love. Before noticing that our toes were the same I felt as if she were a foreigner in my land, in my heart. The toes created this . . . connection. Recognition. Oh, child of mine! This love!

AUGUST

The first time I saw Leora, this creature who was at once half of me, a tenth of my size, and more than I would ever know, I heard this very clear voice in my head: *You must protect her.* I was forty years old and the baby's age was countable in weeks. June pointed out to me so proudly all of the things she could do.

Look, she's holding up her head!

Look, she's smiling!

Look, she's reaching for her toes!

The list was so beautifully basic that it was a reminder of how much of an accomplishment it is that I simply stood, poured myself a glass of water, and drank it while looking out the window as the sun burned the mist from the mountains. What a miracle is life.

I watched the mist for a moment longer as June fed the baby. The rock changed colour dramatically, from a vague and distant blue, the colour of a shadow, to a tarnished gold as the sun broke from the horizon and gilded the rock with its light. My apartment in Chicago had two small windows which simply overlooked the wall of the building next door.

I'm not sure what June had done to make this place feel like a home. It could have simply been her presence, the way she positioned things. There was a warmth to it, a sense that the space was used exactly as it had been designed, with all the required furniture and lamps and plants in just the right places. She had photographs printed and framed. Artwork on the wall. This must have been how she filled her days.

June held the baby to her breast, and after the baby had her fill, June gave her to me. June, lovely June, mother of my child. She had forced me into marriage, made me a baby when I hadn't asked for one, but now I forgave her. In fact, watching her with our daughter began to fill me with this feeling I'd never had before. It was like love, but different. It was like the love I had for my mother mixed with my love for June, but with something else too, something different, that came from an animal place beneath my heart. The feeling of wanting to protect these two girls of mine intensified. I was a little afraid of the feeling.

June seemed quite different to me at first. A shyness had come over her; her body seemed to curve inward on itself, always cradling the baby, feeding the baby, crouched over to dress or change her. She talked less and seemed to listen less, too. She wanted me to speak, to tell her stories of what my work days were like back in Chicago, and I know she was proud of me, but I could tell she was focused on something else when I spoke. She looked out the window, but every few moments glanced down at the baby sleeping at her side. Every few moments June would make a *hmm* sound, as though she were engaged in the story, but she didn't even notice when I asked questions. I didn't hold this against her. She seemed very tired. She was doing such a wonderful job at being a mother. I watched her work at it with admiration. She'd left her job at the hospital several months prior to the birth. The director had told her that patients didn't trust a pregnant woman, and he was probably right. I know that this time filled her with boredom and frustration, but I believed she would flourish with the purpose of motherhood. Perhaps that flourishing would come. It was all still so new.

June gave me Leora so I could take her for a walk, as she wanted to have a bath and prepare dinner. I didn't know how to take a baby for a walk, but it didn't seem like it would be very difficult. People did this all the time. After June had nursed her, she showed me how to tuck the baby into the pram with a blanket and soft elephant toy and pushed us out the door, telling us to have fun. As if a child of this age were able to *have fun.*

Leora's eyes were alert for the first few minutes, and she seemed to take note of all that she could see from her vantage point: sky, leaves on branches, clouds, perhaps birds.

I walked, sometimes watching her, sometimes looking around. I narrated the things that I was seeing, and this felt quite natural, as though I were her teacher.

"There are three people at this crosswalk, Leora, and we are about to cross the road towards them; now they are passing us, and we are approaching the other side, the park, where I imagine you come with your mother most days. It's a lovely day, as you can see. Sunny, not too hot. We're coming up to the fountain, you can hear the sound of the water flowing now."

Soon Leora's eyelids were drooping; she was smiling lazily, contentedly, drunk on the milk of her mother and soothed, perhaps, by the voice of her father. (I was a father! The thought still amazed me.) I started letting my mind drift away from the intense peace of the present moment and towards thoughts of the future. I have always had a forward-thinking mindset, occasionally to my detriment, and I wondered whether having Leora in my life would change this. It didn't: in fact, I think her existence only intensified my focus on the future. I wanted to give her a better world than the one we currently had on offer.

When Leora and I arrived at the park, I took her out of the pram and sat down with her on the bench. She was sleeping soundly, and the movement and ambient sounds did not disturb her. She weighed less than a bag of groceries. I held this perfect baby and my arms felt too bulky and clumsy for her tiny body. I could drop her, easily. I could smother her with my shirt if I held her to my body incorrectly. If I tried, not that I ever would, but of course the vision flashed frightfully for a half-second in my mind, then I could easily break her neck. My body was a dangerous thing. I had created her, and I could destroy her.

JUNE

Parenthood is invisible, and this is why August struggled with it. His life's work was about revealing the shape of invisible forces. Nobody wants to reveal the shape of parenthood. We just want to see its product: a healthy, clean, polite child. Nobody cares about the time one spends feeding the child, rocking her to sleep, watching her sit. Smiling at her. Rubbing her feet because you love those feet, you *are* those feet, they belong to you, but only for so long.

As I said, for my part, I appreciated the privacy. The light playing out on the wall, filtering patterns from the trees outside; the many colours of the sky. Within the first week of Leora's life, I'd seen the sky at every single shade of day. It's blue so little of the time, I wonder why it is that we teach children to call it that. "Blue." It's grey, pink, navy, yellow, black. It's smudged with paint-strokes of gold and purple at dawn and dusk. It's white, like a sheet lit up from behind, when the clouds are there all day but lofted, keeping their distance. It's charcoal at the horizon when a storm is coming. It's mauve on a peaceful morning. The sky is an appropriate metaphor for parenthood. It's vast and changeable and unknowable while also being so fundamental as to be, most of the time, unconsidered.

After she "woke up," I started to play her music. Her reaction was immediate. I put on Mozart's Piano Concerto no. 21 and she abruptly stopped moving. Her head and arms became still, and she got that almost expressionless, focused face she'd worn before her first smile. Like she was trying so hard to learn how to be human. Her tiny eyebrows furrowed, but she appeared completely calm. I'd listened to this piece so many times in the late months of my pregnancy, I wondered whether she recognized it, and remembered. Why wouldn't she? I can hear music through walls; of course she would have heard it through the thin layers of flesh and fluid separating her from the air.

Music was something I shared with August, and it became something I could share with Leora too. I began to keep the radio on almost all of the time. She loved everything equally. I was happy that it gave my mind something to follow that wasn't my own thoughts.

I caught snippets of the war in Europe in this way too. It was difficult to tune that out. I knew August was keeping up with it, as it was relevant to his work, but I found it all so much harder to process now, as I was immobilized with the logistics and emotions of motherhood, and my thoughts of the future were inextricable from the reality of my daughter's life. How will I explain to her—What is war? Why?—when she asks me?

I said that I had no memories of my childhood. I should say that that's not quite correct. At a certain point I let go of all my memories. Remembering anything from back then brings back a grief that I cannot bear, knowing that my parents are gone and nobody but me is here to remember them. The main thing I remember now isn't a thing so much as a feeling. I remember feeling alone, almost all of the time. The solitude was intense. I felt as though my parents didn't understand me. It feels cruel, even sacrilegious to say this now, considering what happened to them, but it's the truth, and I should tell it.

I don't know if adults can ever truly understand children. We leave that perspective, our homelands, behind when we grow up. It happens quite suddenly, and there is no going back. Seeing Leora now, I can only catch glimpses of it. I hope she doesn't feel so alone.

As I cared for my infant I continued to long to have my mother with me, so she could tell me stories of when I was a baby, and hold my baby, and tell me how to do it, tell me it would all be okay. This was before I knew that they were already dead. I wrote to them—of course I did. And then, when the letters were returned, I wrote to a neighbour to ask where they might have moved, but that letter got returned too. I would say in retrospect that I was optimistic, but that's not right. I was just naïve. August didn't seem worried about it, and he was everything for me, the barometer by which I measured and compared my own emotions. So as long as I had him, I reasoned, then I was fine without my parents. I was a grown-up; this was what grown-ups did. It still felt sad, and lonely, but I put the thought of them in a little pocket in my mind and left it there with the hope that they would reach out soon and explain what had happened, where they'd moved. Leora was seven months old when the letters all came back.

Katharine had studied some Chinese medicine for fun, and when she was over for a visit one Saturday afternoon, she asked me to stick out my tongue. I did; Leora copied, her tiny tongue obeying its puppet master. She was six months old, the sweetest thing.

"It's purple," Katharine said of mine, surprised.

"Is it?" I tried to look down to my own tongue and couldn't; I went to see it in the hallway mirror. "Oh." It did have a bruise-like sheen. "What does purple mean?"

"Well, you know I'm new at this, and it's not an exact science, but I believe that purple means you are feeling," she paused, "perhaps a bit stagnant? It represents a deficiency of *chee*," she sounded apologetic, "and the literature says deficiencies can come from, lots of things, like perhaps stress, or trauma, or disappointment."

I felt unpeeled. I tried to choke out a laugh. "Or it could just be the red wine I had with breakfast."

Katharine smiled in this way she had—I could tell she wasn't sure if I was joking.

"Maybe you could get a cat?" she suggested. "Babies need so much. A cat could love you back."

If she couldn't already understand, then I knew it would not be possible for me to explain to her that children love you more than anyone else possibly can, with a love that is irrational and relentless. Their love needs nothing but yours. The way they know your love is primal, too: if their basic needs are met, they know they're loved. How could I tell her I wanted to kiss Leora all day long, to eat her cheeks, to feel her skin on mine?

What I told Katharine, though, was that I didn't want to clean up after a cat.

I loved Leora, so I loved my life, but how is it possible to be happy with something and also wish it was completely different? How is it possible to feel guilty but also know that you'd do the exact same thing again? These seemed to me to be contradictions particular to love, and in my case, to motherhood. I don't know if I'd ever truly known love before motherhood. Not like this.

At fourteen months, Leora took her first steps; by sixteen months, she was "fasting," she called it, as she ran "so fast," and about six weeks after that, she started slowing down. I noticed a limp.

"Sore," she said, holding her left knee after playing with one of her little friends in the park.

"Did you fall?" I crouched down to her level. "Did somebody hurt you?"

"No, no. Hurts the knee." She pointed. Her little eyebrows crumpled. "Pick you up," she said.

She was too young to refer to herself as "I" or "me," still didn't think of herself, or know how to articulate a sense of self, as an independent subject. I'd say, "you want Mama to pick you up?" and the words were a fundamental truth, not fluid pronouns that changed according to the speaker.

"Mama, pick you up," she said again.

"It hurts right here?" I scooped her up, cradling her like a newborn. I gave her a kiss where she pointed, on her kneecap, and I noticed a little bump under my lips. I rubbed it with my fingers. I could feel a nodule under the surface of her skin, about half an inch in diameter. My doctor brain, dormant for so long, suddenly emerged at odds with my mother heart. Something was wrong; nothing was allowed to go wrong. Her knees were only about three inches wide, her bones so tiny, her body still mine; half an inch of something foreign was large in proportion to her smallness. I had a lightning-bolt feeling in my whole body.

I felt her forehead with my cheek; it felt fine, no fever. I asked her to open her mouth; her throat looked fine, not red. Had she been tired? Maybe, but aren't little children always tired? Had she been eating well? Not really, but that hadn't worried me. I'd thought she was cutting her molars.

"Darling, we are going to go to the doctor, all right? To see what's making you sore."

"Nice?" she said.

"Your doctor is so nice, yes, but we will see a different doctor this time. This doctor will also be very nice."

I would take her to Emergency at the hospital rather than try to book an appointment with her family doctor. The lightning bolt told me she needed to be seen right away.

This was the night that my fear, my own narcissistic fear of death, found its true target and took aim. Leora, my Leora.

It was visible on the first X-ray. Right there, so clear. There was no question what it was. The doctor put the picture up on a light box in the small room in which we'd been waiting. I took note of the time, a reflex. 8:59 p.m., December 2, 1942.

Leora was sedated in my arms. They'd had to give her a tranquilizer so she'd stay still for the image-making, and she was bleary with the medication. Had we been at home on a normal schedule she'd have been sleeping already. My girl. I felt so sorry for her losing sleep, focusing on that instead of everything else.

"Oh." I exhaled when I saw it, right there on the left femur, before he'd said anything. My little girl dozing in my lap, unaware except for her sore knee, unable to comprehend the magnitude of what I was coming to realize.

"It's a tumor," the doctor said.

"Yes. I can see that." I pressed my right middle finger to a point in the middle of my right eyebrow, lifting up my eyelid like a tarp that had drooped.

"You're familiar with X-rays, ma'am?"

"I'm a doctor," I said. "I stopped practicing," I nodded towards Leora, "but, yes."

"Right," he said, focused on the present rather than my past, which he seemed to have deemed irrelevant. "And we can see another, smaller one, forming a little further down the shin. Here, see?" He pointed to the bigger tumor, a grape-sized lump at the base of Leora's femur, and then slid his finger down to the other one, smaller than a currant, smaller than a—why is everything always measured in fruit? I hadn't actually seen that one; I felt sick.

"Based on this, and her other presenting symptoms," he continued, too nonchalant, "we have to assume that it is cancer. Of the bone. And it's spreading."

I stroked her leg, first the sick one, then the other.

"So, we'll confirm it first with a biopsy, but in the meantime, I'll book her in for surgery," he said. This man was younger than me. He wore a beard to give him more authority but it had grown in patchy. "Osteosarcoma is aggressive, and unfortunately, I am quite certain that this is what we are dealing with. We'll have to amputate from here."

"It can't be saved?" Her leg. She'd just learned the name for her knee, and now it would be gone.

"It's not worth the risk," he said.

"What's your name, Doctor?" Leora shifted and I adjusted my right arm to support her neck, which was lolling back. She didn't wake.

He looked surprised at the question. "Trunks," he said. "I'm Doctor Mark Trunks."

"And after, Dr. Trunks?" I asked.

"Pardon me?"

"You said we'd *start* with surgery. What comes after?"

"Right," he nodded, crossed his legs. "I'll consult with my team, but we would probably just start there and then, we'd see how it went. We'll make sure we got it all. It's good that it seems to be spreading downwards, at least. The cancer might come back, or it might not, or it might have already migrated to the bloodstream."

As Dr. Trunks was talking, my mind raced, searching through my memories as though hunting for the killer. When had it entered her body? How could I have let this happen? My mind was trying to find the cause for Leora's sickness, my blame within it.

Cancer used to be thought to be contagious. Patients were isolated from their families and communities; hospitals had to be relocated to rural, often coastal, areas. My area of focus was epidemiology, and the various cancer epidemics had been a central point of my research. In 1713, an Italian doctor studied a community of nuns and identified proportionally low incidences of cervical cancer and high incidences of breast cancer and supposed that this might in some way be connected to their celibate lifestyles. And up until quite recently, most doctors believed that cancer was caused by trauma. A tumor in the knee, people thought, could have been caused by a fall. Leora was always falling—but we know now that the trauma theory is far from true. A child—my little girl—has had no lifestyle or occupational risks that could have led to this. She was innocent.

"I just read," I said, my mind finally finding relevant information, "a few months ago, about the first intravenous administration of those, what are they called—chemotherapy drugs? Did you read about that? At Princeton? It came from a form of mustard gas"—I was rambling, but he was listening, so I kept talking—"and when the after-effects of the gas were studied in soldiers, scientists realized that the chemicals had cytotoxic abilities—did you see that? It was in *Nature*. It might mean she could keep her leg, mightn't it? Can we try the drugs? How do we try that?" I might have sounded confident but it felt like I was on my knees, pleading.

This man, this very tall man, sat down. He sighed. "Firstly, I'm sorry about your daughter," he said. "You should take some time. Is your husband at work? You'll want to talk with him, won't you?"

I did not respond.

"Now," he continued, "it's clear you're well-informed, and of course you're well-intentioned, but let me tell you, those drugs are experimental. They're risky. And they were tested on people with blood cancers, an entirely different beast to solid cancers. We don't have authorization to use them here, outside of that clinical trial you read about, and I would not advise waiting to proceed with treatment."

August would have fought. Would August have fought?

"Right," I said. "I will talk to my husband."

When I said that, it felt as if I was trying to prove that we had options, that we were not desperate. Why did I want to imply this? Desperate was exactly what I was. We had no options. There was nothing I could have done differently that would have led to a different outcome. And there was nothing

I could do to protect her. If this doctor told me I had to stay in the hospital forever, that I would never bring my daughter home again, that chopping off her leg immediately and then remaining within these walls for constant monitoring was her only chance at survival, of course I would have done that. But he did not say that. He simply nodded. Was I meant to make an appointment? Should I get a second opinion? Americans always seem to think that one doctor's diagnosis might be different from another's, as though medicine is a practice of subjectivity rather than a search for objective truth; as though doctors are simply people with opinions.

I stopped by the post office on the way home, leaving Leora sleeping in the car for a moment, to send him a telegram.

She's sick, I wrote. *Cancer of the bone.*

Chicago is one hour ahead of Denver, so I figured he would already be asleep and would not receive my message until the morning. I wanted him with me. Of the things I was allowed to wish for that might possibly come true, this was the one thing I let myself want.

AUGUST

There have been moments in my life where all of the many possible decisions for the future are, in an instant, stripped away and distilled into a single, obvious choice, even if it is a difficult one. I felt this way when I received the telegram.

I'd returned from the lab in the early hours of the morning. The whole walk home had passed in an instant; it felt as though I was floating, my mind high as a kite, my thoughts travelling at the speed of light. It was still dark, but there was a clarity to the air. This was the night of our successful experiment. We had just changed the world; I was aglow.

And then, I saw the envelope.

She was sick. Cancer of the bone. It didn't say who "she" was, but the telegram was from June—there was only one possibility. I instantly sank back down to the ground, and my heart went deeper still. The rest of my world—the experiment, my work, my career—fell aside, like an avalanche of snow falling from the cliff, revealing the shape of an entirely new mountain. My Leora.

I poured myself a glass of water and sat down at the tiny dinette in my kitchen, in which I never cooked a thing. I ate out. I snacked. I filled the fridge with cured meats, pickles, and cakes. Leora. The last time I'd seen her was three months before, when I was visiting for a weekend in the summer. Perhaps it had been more like five months, then. I could see her tiny face when I closed my eyes. Her wispy waves of sand-coloured hair. Her eyes, dark brown, like pebbles in a river. Her face when she was concentrating; the way her cheeks dimpled when she laughed. She was confident on her feet but still loved to be held. With hardly any syllables, she managed to explain to her mother or me the particular way in which she desired to be touched: for my two hands to hold each of her feet and squeeze them, to be held close and rocked like a little baby, or to sit up on my shoulders and hold my ears as if they were the reins of a horse. She lit up whenever her beautiful mother walked into the room, as though June was the only light she needed in the world.

I went to the travel agent first thing in the morning and he booked me onto the next departing flight to Denver. I don't even remember how much the ticket cost.

After that, I went straight to the lab. "I am leaving this afternoon," I told Antonio. "I have to go home." I don't think I'd ever referred to Denver as *home*.

He was making coffee in his silver Bialetti stovetop pot. He had such a particular routine of it: he used only distilled water and imported Italian beans. "We've only just begun," he said, giving me a cup. "There is much to be done."

The coffee was strong, which was how I liked it. I hadn't slept at all that night.

"There is much to be done, yes, but not by me. I am no longer needed here."

I brought the coffee to my office to see what papers I might want to bring with me. My office had no windows to the outside world, but it did have a large window looking onto the lab, where we had just the night before completed our experiment. It felt unreal, that it was only hours ago. People were back down there already, or perhaps they hadn't even left, taking notes of the final readings of the radioactivity. Some had started cleaning up. I saw E. P. there, scrubbing on his hands and knees, bless him. The black graphite had gotten into everything.

I had many notebooks full of writing, measurements, and diagrams I had made over the years, preparing for the day before. And now it was finished. I had done it, and I was leaving. It all felt quite far away now. I sat down at my desk and idly flicked through my paperwork when Antonio came in without knocking.

"What's going on, August?"

I leaned back. The news so far existed only for me and June. As far as I knew, other than the doctor, nobody else knew that Leora was sick. She probably didn't even know herself.

I savoured this last moment that Antonio still thought of my daughter as healthy and untarnished—or even, that he didn't think of her at all.

"Leora, my daughter, has cancer," I said. "I am going to Colorado for a while to be with her and June."

"Oh, no." He pulled up my spare chair.

"I found the telegram when I got back to my apartment last night. It's in the bone."

"August, I'm so sorry. How long will you stay for?" Antonio finished his coffee.

"I'll have to see." Denver still felt foreign to me, but uncertainty, and indefiniteness, felt familiar.

I didn't want to talk to Antonio, but I was glad he was there. "Glad" might be too strong a word. It felt pleasant to have the presence of another. We weren't close, really, even as colleagues—we had fundamental disagreements over many of the moral aspects of science—but, if I thought about it, I didn't really have anyone I was close to. I had no friends in Chicago, or Denver. I had people with whom I spent time in New York, people who invited me to dinners and parties, but nobody I wanted to write to or call to talk about this, or even about the success of our experiment the night before.

One of the students last night had taken photographs; he was probably developing them now. How would the interplay of light and shadow be captured by a medium that only pictured light and shadow?

"It is a shame to have to leave now," I said then, looking out over our lab.

"Your work will go on." He gripped my hand in a very loving gesture and held it for just a half second. "While I have you, I was thinking of what elements we might use to experiment with next. Have you had any thoughts?"

"Well"—I hadn't had any thoughts specifically, but I let thoughts come: "What if we did something with the neutrons in the pile beyond measuring them? We were treating the manganese as a radioactive nuisance to be disposed of, but what if we could use it instead? What if we could activate other elements?"

"Hmm," he nodded.

"I think cobalt would be interesting to try," I said, off the cuff.

He looked quite impressed by all this. "Interesting. Cobalt. Interesting."

I've not often found conversation to be a generative place for me—most of my thinking happens alone, in the fluid motion of walking, or dreaming, or doing nothing at all—but, perhaps with the knowledge of my imminent departure, and the excitement of the night before, and the sudden chasm I felt between life and death, speaking with Antonio was opening up ideas within me. As a metal, cobalt is silver-grey with a slight blue tinge in certain lights, which is why it was called by the Germans *kobold*—"goblin" ore. It becomes its famous deep bright blue only when oxidized and dehydrated.

"When did you think of all this?" Antonio continued.

"Just now, really. Just thinking."

He nodded, discerning.

"I'll see if I can do any research while I'm down there," I said, not believing I would have either the time or the desire. "It would be interesting to see if the leftover neutrons might be of some use, somehow. So that we're not just producing toxic waste."

Knowing what we know about cobalt now, with all the tests I've conducted and useful inventions I've brought into this world, I'm honestly a little surprised that I'm not in Sweden instead of the Netherlands, waiting to be awarded with the Nobel Prize in Physics instead of being tried for war crimes. Context is everything.

Cancer research and treatments were still fairly rudimentary then, and the disease was almost always fatal, no matter where it was growing. In the months and years since Leora's diagnosis, I've changed this. I like to think my invention has given many people hope, and I'm hoping that will balance things in my favour tomorrow. While it's true that the cobalt bomb will kill many, this is only a hypothetical: my cobalt machine has already saved so many lives. What do you think is more important to consider in the scope of my guilt? Possibility, or reality? We'll get to the machine soon, but you know she's alive, and I assure you: it's because of me.

JUNE

Leora and I got a taxi to meet him at the airport—I think he'd forgotten we would, because he seemed surprised we were there—and when he walked through the doors I could tell he hadn't slept. He looked like a spent match, but some fire sparked in him when he saw us, which lit me up too. He was only forty-one but his handsome face was drooping, as if the skin was melting around the bottom. We hugged, and I fell into his softness, his smell; I could smell the shower he'd had that morning but also the sweat of stress, travel, strain. I can't describe how it felt to be near someone who had become almost imaginary in the surreal abstraction of the past few days. We say "larger than life," what does that mean? There has always been a largesse to August, but he encompassed my whole life within his breadth.

He was home. We were together. Our family of three.

He said he would stay indefinitely. I didn't let go of his hand.

We developed rhythms of intimacies quickly. He asked questions of the doctors. He did the dishes. He swallowed my grief. Despite being the saddest I've ever been, in some ways this time was also the happiest. When we had sex, it's not like we expected or even wanted to conceive another child, but it felt like we were trying to make Leora unbroken, to create and give birth to her healthy self all over again.

AUGUST

I felt unlike myself. What is a self, in these circumstances? Was I thinking about who I had been during my childhood— quiet, and nervous, but cared for—longing to return to some projection of a prelapsarian state? I wished I could talk to my mother, be held by her with the love that could protect me. I wished I could be with my brother, but we had lost touch, I didn't know even where he lived. I called my father, who lived in Queens, New York. He had never even met his grand-daughter. He was frail; we were busy.

"Oh, Leo," my father said. He had called me Leo since I was a little boy, I think because those born in August have the star sign of Leo; and though I've never known my father to take any interest in astrology, I can think of no other reason. I wish I'd asked. "I'm so sorry."

I just held the phone to my ear. I felt so far away. How I longed to be parented.

"How long does she have?" he continued. He spoke sensitively, it wasn't some mechanical statement, but the question, the reality, was just so brutal that it broke the one soft part of my heart that must have still remained unbroken.

"That's not how it is," I responded quickly, as if scolding him, to cover up the emotion that rose in my throat. "I will make sure she has forever."

"Of course," he said. He paused, and I could hear him thinking. "It is very hard as a parent to outlive your child, Leo. After you three were born, your mother and I wanted to be there with you forever, you know. She said she couldn't bear the thought of any of you dying alone, but then again, she couldn't bear the thought of being there, either."

"I will make sure you get to meet her," I said. "I'm so sorry we haven't been out to visit yet."

"Leo, I love you," he said, for what might have been the first time. And then he hung up. That was the last time we spoke. He never met my daughter.

I had been back in Denver for a week and was beginning to get to know Leora again. She was a delight. She was her own little self, suddenly. I didn't take her love of me as a given, but she was so eager to give it to me. She stilled in my arms as soon as I picked her up, and she nuzzled her tiny body into mine.

"Dada," she said, touching my upper lip, then gently round the edges of my nostrils. "Dada came back."

We went for a walk together one afternoon, the three of us. Leora was quiet in her pram. June and I were quiet too. I was pushing the pram, and after we'd been walking for a little while, June stopped and stooped down to Leora's level.

"Darling, are you all right?"

Leora nodded.

"Are you happy?"

"No."

June tensed. "Are you sad?"

"No."

"What are you feeling, sweetheart?" June seemed to be begging—for something, I don't know what.

Leora looked at the trees, and said: "I be relax."

It struck me that joy and sorrow are binaries we project upon children, expecting them to always be vacillating between these two poles, and yet Leora had presented a third option. She could be neither of those things and still content, not having any needs.

June looked up at me, her eyes like oceans. We walked the rest of the way home in silence.

I asked her doctors for three months so that I could research treatments before they took her leg. They said I could have ten days, which was the same as nothing. Still, I threw myself into it. I made notes during dinner at the kitchen table. I took long walks whenever I felt my thoughts stagnate. I stayed up late and slept in to make up for my insomniac wanderings.

On a walk one evening I noticed the mountains turned blue at a distance, at the border of what could be seen. I knew that if I were ever to get close, the blue would transform into its true colours: grey rock, brown earth, emerald foliage. Blue is the colour of the distance, not the object. Blue is the colour of where you are not.

I thought of the night we had conducted the experiment in Chicago. It was only a couple of weeks ago and it felt like a story someone had told me. I felt drawn to that story; I wanted it to be told to me, the way my mother used to tell me those stories of good and evil when I was a young boy.

When the uranium atom is split, the remaining pieces are highly unstable. In nature, anything that is unstable longs for stability, and will emit as much energy as necessary in order to find a stable form. We call this phenomenon "radioactivity," which means, etymologically, motion in the outer radius. Marie Curie was the first to call it this, and she used the term to refer to the mysterious elements-emitting particles she worked with. She knew about x-rays, and knew that uranium emitted these x-rays, but she and her husband Pierre wanted to figure out where this "radioactivity" was coming from. When she and her husband refined some uranium metal from the ore, to everyone's surprise, they found that the leftover ore showed more activity of the x-rays than the pure uranium metal, proving that radioactivity wasn't just a strange quirk of uranium, but a common feature of the natural world.

So, I can imagine my younger self asking, is Marie *good*? Is radioactivity *good*?

There is no such thing as *good* when we talk about people, I know, for so much exists in a grey area. But I still find myself drawn to the stark divisions of this concept of morality. Marie was good and also cheated on her husband, perhaps driving him to his tragic death. Her intimacy and obsession with her work led to her own death, too; her body is still radioactive. Radioactivity is neither good nor bad but can be involved in both creation and destruction. It can kill and it can heal, it can be toxic as well as generative, but as a concept, it is as neutral as a sock. Good and evil is an observation that depends on who has the power, and in whom you believe.

Leora's body had become—well, I suppose you could say it had become unstable. Life generally wants to live, and her body, and her little self, wanted to return to stability. I couldn't think of her condition as one that had previously been good and had now become bad: this notion of a fall from grace implies a morality that is not true here. She had done nothing. She was still perfect within her deteriorating body.

I'd told Antonio that I thought cobalt would make an interesting candidate for nuclear activation, and I'm not sure where my instincts came from there, but I had this strong feeling. Could something come from this experiment for Leora too? We knew the isotope Cobalt-59 to be stable, but if an extra neutron were added, it would become Cobalt-60, an extremely radioactive isotope. Instead of irradiating uranium with neutrons, what if we irradiated cobalt instead, and instead of harnessing the general energy, harnessed the radiation? Neutrons make alchemy possible. This sounds metaphorical, and it might be, but it is also literal. With neutrons we can turn one element into another. It's not as magical or pure as the alchemists from eighth-century Arabia had imagined, because in transforming the element it becomes radioactive, and produces all kinds of other things in the process that are generally not desirable. But this is as close as we can get to alchemy. And cobalt is blue, the blue of distance, of longing, the blue of being over there instead of right here. I saw it. Out of the blue. I could picture it so clearly. But there was no way I could create this radiation machine I imagined in my remaining four days before Leora's surgery.

By the time I got back to the house after my walk, it was very dark. The smear of the Milky Way was visible beyond the rooftops. Most of the lights in the windows of the neighbourhood had been turned out.

June had made a roast chicken for dinner, stuffed with lemons and fresh rosemary, with carrots and mashed potatoes whipped with cream. Leora was already sleeping, the table set only for two. June lit candles. There was wine. She was wearing a nice dress. The soft, papery skin around her eyes was more pronounced, and I wondered whether it was the candlelight, or if she'd been crying, or if she always looked this way and I just hadn't noticed.

"Am I late?" I asked. "I'm sorry, I didn't realize."

"Didn't realize it was late, or didn't realize I would feed you?"

I didn't think she intended for the question to be answered. "This looks delicious, thank you, June."

"Where did you go?"

"I'm not sure," I said. "I think I might have gotten a bit turned around."

We ate, and drank wine, and then sat on the couch.

"I had an idea, for Leora." As I told her about it, I think she forgave me.

"I think that the experiment we just conducted will lead to—could be used to develop—a machine that will treat Leora's cancer, and all cancers. It could cure them."

"Now?"

"Not right now, of course, there's research, testing, building, and that takes years, but—"

"If you can't invent and build this machine in four days, then how will you cure Leora?"

I took a sip of my wine and let out a big breath. June and I were thinking in different time frames. She has always been someone more able to immerse herself in the present, while I think in seasons, in projects, in lifetimes. There are pros and cons to each approach. I do believe that she feels trapped in the present, at times. Unable to visualize herself out of a bad feeling, to know that it is as fleeting as a breath. I felt a need to apologize for getting her hopes up but also for what I was about to do: cut them down further.

"Cancers of this nature have the tendency to recur, unfortunately, so—"

"I don't want to talk about recurrence, August. I just want to live here, right now, forever."

"Sweetheart. June. You know that you can't put *now* in front of *more*."

June had left her family, and then lost them. This was colouring her views, and I regret not giving her the sympathy I should have. She started to cry, and I thought that I could fix it by telling her more about my machine; and that might have helped at a different time, when she could see with her rational brain, but at the moment, the fog of feeling was clouding her vision.

"Please don't make this about work," she said. "We have four days to enjoy her before her surgery. Just let this be about us."

"I can work on this idea over the next several months, or years, and maybe—hopefully—Leora will never need it, and it will cure the cancers of other people, but if she does, I will make sure it's ready for her."

June's shoulders sloped forward, reaching for one another.

"June. This will be such a revolution. When I can make it work, and I really believe that I can, then it will save countless lives. It will allow people to live in hope instead of in fear. It will completely change the way we perceive of cancer—it won't be a death sentence any more than an infection is. I can see the through-line of the nuclear research we've been doing in a way I couldn't before: there's this feeling of it being part of a bigger picture, bigger even than a bomb—it will be—"

"So it's not even for Leora? It's for the whole world?"

"June," I said, looking at her eyes, so exhausted. "Come on."

"I suppose you have always been this way," she said. "I just hoped that, with a family of your own, you would change."

Oh, it is hard to go over all of this. Nostalgia is a painful place to be—the pain of never being able to go back to that place we called home. Is that what these dull little rooms are for? So that those held captive are forced to go into their past, to mull over what could have been different?

The days did pass, whatever we did with them, and Leora did lose her leg, and I don't think June ever forgave me.

Of course I have regrets! So many regrets! I regret, most of all, that I wasn't able to convince June of . . . that I wasn't able to communicate . . . I don't know how to say it. That I didn't treat her better. But I do not regret saving my daughter's life. Could I have been more present? June would say yes, but I'm not sure. Could I have been more loving? I thought I had been loving, but it wasn't in the ways she needed. I'm not saying it's all her fault.

JUNE

After the surgery, the doctors came out of the operating room and told us that they got all the cancer. It was gone. When we took her home a few days later—they'd wanted to monitor her for thirty-six hours—I felt such joy that we were only bringing our baby back, and not the monster that had been eating her bones.

She didn't seem to miss her foot, or ankle, or calf, or knee. I watched her face like a spy. The drugs must be working, I thought, as she didn't seem to be in pain. She took delight in the same things she always had. She ate, she laughed, she seemed normal—the same, but without half of her left leg. We carried her, which she'd insisted on much of the time beforehand anyway, but she also quickly fashioned a new type of crawling motion, using the strength of her arms to pull her body along behind her, and using her right leg as a sort of tripod to lift herself up.

Leora slept in the bed between August and I the night that she came home. For many nights after, too.

"Cuddle big bed," she said, smugly, nuzzling with her stuffed elephant; smug because she knew that she was in charge, and that we would obey.

I kept the curtains open a little bit to let some light in. The shadows of the bare winter trees waved over the green ferns on the wallpaper, like a tiger was moving through the jungle undergrowth. I had to be alert. I had let my guard down and the cancer had snuck through, but I would not allow any more predators to pass.

August and I lay there on either side of her, not speaking for a few minutes. Our breaths were in three different rhythms, and within moments, Leora's slowed to the pace of dreams. Her belly inflated with one last big breath and then her inhales became shallow, regular. Her fingers twitched, like anemones in a current. She always fell asleep so quickly, an instant letting-go. She had such trust in the world, that it would be there when she returned, and in us, to stay and watch over her.

If it was only the two of us, Leora and I, I would often stay in bed and eventually fall asleep myself. My sleep was always shallow when she was by my side, watchful for dangers I was able to put out of my mind if she was in her own bed; but still, it seemed important, and worth the sacrifice, to have her near.

But with August there, it was different. After she'd been breathing steadily for a few minutes, he lifted his head from the pillow, met my eyes, and nodded in the direction of the door.

"Meet you there," I mouthed, as he left.

I wanted to stay for a bit longer. I put my hand on her chest; she didn't stir. It had now been four days since the surgery, and I wanted to look underneath the dressing that was taped down above her knee. I lifted the layers of white gauze until they became patterned with rust-coloured circles, like the imprints of waves. She did a shuddering, shuffling sigh, but kept sleeping, so I kept going. I knew the leg was gone, of course, but I hadn't yet seen what, exactly, remained. When all of the gauze was gone, I saw that what was left, what was visible, was what had previously been on the inside of her body. At least, that's how it looked to me. The skin was struck through with red lines. There was blood, and it was scabbing. The black surgical stitching was visible, as if she was wearing a shirt inside out. What had they done with the rest of her leg? Would it be buried? Burned? Studied? Why hadn't they asked me what I wanted done?

I didn't touch the wound. Her whole body felt like it belonged to me, but this part did not. My baby.

After examining it, I taped the pieces of gauze back down and went to find August, quietly pulling the door shut behind me. I pushed my hair behind my ears and rubbed my tongue along my teeth. I was not going to tell him what I had done, what I had seen. I still felt a little shy around him sometimes.

The room was dark, and neither of us reached for the lights. There was still enough light coming through the windows: the last of the sun bouncing off the mountains, from the street lamps' electric glow. There was an equilibrium between the outside and the inside, and perhaps that was what we didn't want to break. Soon the light would dim outside, soon we would turn on the lamps, and light the fire, but for now, there was this cozy feeling of being suspended. The shadows on his face made him look almost unrecognizable, and then light would shift, and he would emerge again. The smell of the potted hyacinth I'd bought, its tiny pink buds just beginning to bubble, filled the room with the smell of cheap champagne.

"This is nice," I said. It really did feel nice. I was able to find a bottle of red and the corkscrew without turning on the lights in the kitchen.

"Here." I handed August his glass.

And then, the equilibrium tipped. August reached for a lamp, and the top half of his face was cast in bronze, the lower half, covered in stubble, still the colour of shadows. "It is nice," he agreed.

"How does she seem to you?" I asked him. I had a sip of my wine.

He thought about it. I watched him, waiting for his response, and noticed some hair inside of his ears.

"She has accepted this without question, as though it's what we're having for dinner." He drank. "She will be just fine," he said.

It didn't seem real until he said it. My instinct was to thank him. If he said this, he must think that it would never come back, that she wouldn't relapse. I was the doctor, but he was the one with authority. I trusted him.

He got some kindling and matches and lay the logs in the fireplace in some calculated formation. I finished my glass.

For the first time in a while I didn't go to the window to see what the neighbours were doing, if anyone was out for a walk or on their way somewhere. Though all was certainly not perfect in the world, my family was here, and everyone was fine. I could focus, if I wanted to, on the life in front of me instead of the death that lingered around the margins.

"I've been thinking a lot about my idea," he said, "the machine. I really think that it will work."

"That's nice," I said, not really paying attention, feeling this new happiness settle through my body as the wine reached the tips of my fingers. I was remembering what it had felt like to fall in love with August, how I'd loved him even before I met him. I had fallen in love with his mind, with his letters, with the idea of him. Perhaps it was no wonder, then, that the bulk of our relationship happened off-stage, in between different cities, sometimes different countries. Our love was never something I could forget. People say doubt makes them more faithful, better believers, whatever it is that they believe. I felt the same way about love.

"That means I'm going to go back to Chicago soon. I need to get started." He took a big inhale, then let it go. "If the cancer comes back, I need to be ready."

I shook my head. "You're leaving?" I kept shaking my head. I was on the couch but it felt like I was floating away, carried by the wind.

"June," he said.

"But they got it all, they said so. The cancer is gone."

"For now, yes."

I didn't say anything. If I said something, I would cry.

"You didn't think I'd stay forever, did you?"

But the thing is, I had. "You said indefinitely."

"That's not the same as forever. I have to make money, darling."

The way he said *darling* made it seem like I was nobody's darling. It was impatient, bordering on contemptuous. He could make money doing anything he wanted. He knew that. If he wanted to live his life here with us, with his family, he could get a job at the university here instantly, or perhaps even at a private laboratory, or hospital, or government agency of some kind. He had options, is what I'm trying to say, though the way he saw his life, it followed only one path.

I thought marriage had rules, and I had behaved accordingly. Just like the night, marriage was something one must obey, or try to. But all along, August had been making his own rules. He had been happy with that. Maybe he would have been happier had I also done the same from the start.

"How long will you be gone?"

He sighed in that way he does, like I was a child asking impossible questions. He turned to the fire. If he leaned back, he would have rested on my shins. He did not lean back.

"Why don't we come with you, then?" I said. "If this work will take a long time, Leora and I could come to Chicago. Right?"

He said nothing.

I kept swimming into the silence. "I know you'll be working a lot, but at least we will be together, as a family. We can have mornings together, and I can make dinner, whenever you come home. It would be so good—for Leora."

He looked at me with this confused expression. He still didn't say anything.

My last argument: "It's not like I have a job to keep me here anymore."

"But her doctors are here," he said, "her treatment."

"The surgery is over. She can see doctors in Chicago for any follow-up." I couldn't believe that I was pleading with him. I thought he'd be delighted at my idea, that he would see it like I did: as a problem solved.

"There's no room," he said, "my apartment there is so small."

I laughed. "We can find a bigger apartment! Or a house, in the suburbs. We can sell this one, get a family home out there." I was starting to get excited about the idea. I loved my mountains, but I didn't like my life.

"June." He reached back and held onto my kneecap like it was a gearshift. "We're better like this. This is the way it's always been. It's easier for me to keep my work and my family separate. I need to focus when I'm there."

Disbelief has a numbing quality, similar to abandonment. There's always the thought—the hope—that the thing you're imagining will not happen. The hope vanishes surprisingly slowly.

"My brain isn't good at going into different modes like that," he continued. "I live in my work when I'm there, I hardly even come up for air."

"Then change," I said. "Practice. Get better at it!"

He cocked his chin, like a dog listening for a sound.

"Or don't! Don't change, and it'll just be fine as it is!" I didn't realize my voice was getting louder.

"I don't like it when you get like this."

"Like what? I'm your wife. You're my husband. You're her *father*. We should—we should at least be together."

I hated him, but still I wanted him.

"I know it might seem that way to you, June. And I wish it was that simple for me, too."

"Might *seem?* Might *seem?* What, our family is only an illusion for you?"

He stood up, brushed off the fronts of his pants. "Contain yourself, June." He went to the window, and the tether that tied us together grew taut.

"Or else what? You'll *leave me?* You're already gone."

You'll probably think that I was this stereotypical housewife—I'm sure the neighbours did—but I had been his equal, and now I had fallen. I worry how this will be perceived during the trial. Nobody pities a housewife but everyone identifies with her, and that is why they push her away. We don't want to see that. It's not just boring—it's terrifying.

"If you're going to make money off Leora," I said abruptly, not knowing what I was going to say until I said it, "then you need to give it to her. To us."

I didn't know then that this thought would lead us to where we are now.

"Darling," he said again. Less impatient this time. More contempt.

"I want you here," I interrupted. "Or I want to be there. I just want us to be together, and if you won't agree to that, then I need . . . something else."

He took a deep breath. "You don't know what you want."

My whole body burned, and I was about to scream, forgetting our sleeping baby, but before I could open my mouth, he kept going.

"I want Leora to live," he said. "If this is what you want too, then you will see that I must go."

"When is it that you became so cold?"

"My dear June." He came a little closer. "You know me to have an objective mind. Objectivity is not the same as coldness. I am thinking of our daughter." I could feel his eyes looking all over my face, my chin, my temples, my lips. "And one might say that the person making marriage a financial arrangement is the cold one."

"No," I said, quietly, "*I* am thinking of our daughter. *I* am with her every minute of every day, washing her hair and wiping her hands and making her food and picking her up and teaching her how to understand this world. And what she will understand is that her father left her."

"June."

I was so angry, I was just so angry. Anger turned inwards becomes bitterness. Sometimes it takes generations, sometimes it happens in an instant. The bitterness rose up to my throat so that it was all I tasted when I swallowed air. All I wanted was him. It hadn't necessarily been that way from the beginning. As I've said, in a way, I had enjoyed my freedoms in the early years of our relationship. We had been almost bohemian. Bohemian Jewish refugee scientists. But when Leora came, my role changed, and so too did my dynamic with August. She brought permanence. I needed to make choices, and any choice comes with sacrifices no matter how much you gain.

"She doesn't need another person to love her the way you do," he said. "You are doing enough. You are all she needs there. I love her in a different way."

"I can't see your love. Neither can she. And if she can't see it, then for her, it doesn't exist. She's a baby, August, you don't understand anything about children. All that she needs is her father to be there for her."

"Maybe you're right, maybe I don't know about babies, but I do know about humans, and life, and death. I know what can happen, and I know I need to do this for Leora."

"Fine. So go. And send me money, more money, so I can give her a good life."

"This research is not funded, June." He held out his hands. "Nobody is asking for it, nobody is paying for it."

"If you think people will need it, then people will pay for it. Figure it out." I stood up and left the room.

I lay in the bed next to Leora. I could feel my blood in my face. My eyes were wide open, looking at everything between my nose and the ceiling. I took a big, shuddering breath, and tried to slow the pace of my breath to match hers. She had slept through it all.

August didn't come to bed. I waited, thinking he would, believing he'd come to apologize, to kiss me, make love to me.

He always goes away, but he always comes back. He isn't the type to hold a grudge—emotions don't affect him the way they do me. They pass over him, like water in a stream. The fight was bad, but I would have forgiven him. But he didn't come back. He slept on the couch that night, and he left a few days later.

Leora was fine, but she was also not fine. She could become not fine at any moment. She had all the needs of a toddler, plus all those of someone who had just lost a leg. I couldn't focus on anything, and I also couldn't leave the house. I watched Leora all the time, as if I really could catch any cancer cells before they latched upon her again.

While she slept, and I had "free time," I had to force my mind to think about something else. The doctors disregarded my medical opinions, August disregarded my identity, so I tried to find some place to burrow my busy heart. I started going deeper into my own research of patent law; I thought it might be a way to help with the hospital bills. August had so many ideas he hadn't fully realized: one of them might be worth something. I went through his archives, which were stored with me at the Colorado house. His address in Chicago never felt permanent, and he was often travelling, so he put my house (though perhaps we still considered it "our house" back then) for the return address. I already had the newspaper clippings; it wasn't much more work to manage everything together. There was so much in there. He was a bit of a dilettante, and in reading through all of his research notes I learned so much—about his work, but also about him. I hadn't quite grasped the depth of his ambition and I was struck by his combination of altruism and narcissism. Just as he'd said at that first dinner we had together, he wanted to make the world a better place—and to be celebrated for doing so.

By the time the cobalt situation came up, I knew just what I was doing; of course I did.

I am June. I told you I wasn't involved in anything to do with the bomb. That wasn't exactly true. I didn't have anything to do with making the *atomic* bomb, but the fact that the cobalt bomb was made—well, I'm sure that would have happened eventually, regardless.

AUGUST

A bomb is a symbol of hubris, of pride towards or defiance against the gods. The man with the bomb is stronger than any god, for he has rewritten the laws of the universe. I've never made a bomb, and it is important to remember that I didn't invent the bomb *first*. I was the first, yes, but that vision was secondary to the process of the chain reaction at the nuclear level of the cell, and it was only after my discovery of a cure for cancer that I conceived of the cobalt bomb. If I'm incriminated for this, it will imply that the cure wasn't worth it.

My name is August. I tried my best.

The night has reached its hinge: the hours since the sun has fallen are equal to the time it will take for light to return. I am in the middle. I am not alone, I am sure, in my state of wakefulness. The night is full of us.

I can hear the wind making instruments of the thin trees. I can hear the water, the way it jumps up on the rocks. Do I hear the wind and the water? Or do I only hear the way they interact with solid matter? There is a difference. The earth has so much to say and I don't often listen.

After Leora's operation and I was back in Chicago, I began developing the machine I had envisioned to cure her. It was my job to bring this machine to life, and to save hers. They were two goals, but twinned. I had lost something when I'd discovered nuclear fission, when my dreams of this providing some sort of global salvation, with clean energy, were thwarted. Manipulated. As soon as the idea was released into the hands of others, clean energy became less important than a dirty bomb. I had the chance to do this again, with a better ending, with my radiation machine. My two legacies: my work, and my daughter. It was a common goal, for a common good.

As I worked, I felt as if I was underwater, no light penetrating to my depths. What little light I had to see by was almost gelatinous; my ideas were slow-moving and dull. I felt all of my work on a deeply personal level, I always have, but the implications of this research within my own life were overwhelming. It was so difficult to move forward because I wanted it so badly. Setbacks felled me. Hope was harder than it had ever been.

I had no grant to pursue this new project, nobody wanted it of me, and yet I was investing all my personal time and limited finances into the pursuit. June was siphoning off more than I kept for myself. My mood had turned harshly dour and I began to worry about my own fate as well as mankind's.

There were rumours in our community that Jews were being killed in Germany under Hitler's Nazi regime. It wasn't in the news, but friends of friends were saying that people they knew were disappearing. Einstein had written to me about it; other Jewish colleagues here had heard murmurs, too. *Extermination* was the word, whispered like a nightmare. Rounded up in their homes and shipped off on trains, no sign of where.

And what could I do? I gave all my knowledge on the nuclear reactors to the Americans, hoping that this would ensure that our country was at least as well armed as Germany. I consulted with my colleagues and my leaders as best as I could, but I had this terrible feeling that nothing would be enough.

The underwater feeling came less from what was going on in the outside world, despite all of the intense tragedies that I knew surrounded me, and more, I confess, from the well of sadness within me: I feared that I would not make progress with my radiation machine, that even if I could, attacking cancer was not enough, for the disease was nothing compared to the cancer the Nazis were spreading. The tidal force of guilt crashed onto me constantly: nothing I could do would be enough for Leora, for my family, for humanity.

One morning, coming up for air, I stood up from my desk and went downstairs to the foyer to get the mail. The first post would have just arrived.

There was the *Tribune* and the *Times* and an envelope that looked official, and so I opened it right away: Antonio and I had been awarded a patent for co-designing the first nuclear reactor. A patent! Antonio had handled the application, I had forgotten about it. And now! A patent like this would certainly yield a large amount of money, as this machine would be used all over the world. This! This could help fund my new research!

I floated on top of the water for a moment upon thinking of this, and how it would change my days.

The cost of long-distance phone calls normally deterred me, but now, joyful and rich, I went back up to my undomesticated apartment, took the phone off the hook, sat at the dinette table, and called June.

"It's me," I said, when she picked up.

"August? What's wrong?"

"Nothing's wrong, what do you mean? Is everything all right there? How's Leora?" She'd worried me.

"She's fine, we're fine," then there was a muffled sound as she covered the mouthpiece and I could hear her speaking, but not her words. "It's just that you never call, I thought there might be an emergency."

"No emergency, no. What are you doing right now?" I asked.

"I'm watching Leora take all the books off the shelf in the sitting room," she said. "She's always trying to climb up the shelf so she can see out the window. She likes to watch the cars go by."

"Does she often succeed?"

"I never let her."

"Is she eating well? Does she seem to be in pain?"

"Yes, and no. Sometimes when she wakes up her face is damp and flushed and she says *Ora sore*, and points to the place where her knee used to be, and I think she must have had a dream, or remembered what the pain used to feel like. Or maybe it's those 'phantom' pains people talk about. She's two, it's hard to know what she can remember, or what she's capable of feeling, and the limits her language imposes on her expression of that."

"Yes," I said, "I know the feeling." Learning German, and learning English, had made me feel like a colt learning to use its legs.

"But she is such a happy little girl, she laughs at everything. Did you know that for young children fear registers the same as delight? Both are a good kind of surprise. I see that in her all the time." There was a muffled sound and I heard June say *Leora, stop that please.*

"Do you want to say hello to her?"

"Oh, of course." I hadn't really thought that would be possible. We'd never talked on the phone before.

I heard some background scuffling, June telling Leora that

it was her daddy on the phone, and then, her tiny, happy voice: "Dada?"

"Hello, my baby girl!" I could hear how the smile changed my voice. "I miss you."

"Dada! Missoo, missoo, missoo! Soft the knee!"

"What are you up to, Leora? Are you making a big mess?"

"Hello Dada! Bye-bye Dada!" she said, laughing, and then I heard cloth against the mouthpiece as Leora dropped the phone, communication and distance two incompatibly abstract notions for a toddler, and then June was on the line again.

"I was actually calling," I said, excited, "because I have good news!" I told her about the letter I'd just received, how I anticipated that this patent would amount to over a year's worth of full-time research and development for the radiation machine. There would likely even be enough money to build a prototype.

"So you're just going to—to use up all of the money for your work?"

"For . . . Leora."

"Right, right. Because none of this is for you." Her voice was laced with a sudden contempt, which terrified me. "Do you remember what you told me that first night we went to dinner?"

I did not remember. All I remembered was the warm feeling of being near her.

"What do you want, June?" I paid all the bills on the house.

I gave her a generous weekly allowance. "You have your free-dom," I said.

"You know how I feel about freedom."

There was silence on the line for a few moments. That silence probably cost me three dollars.

"Listen," I said finally, "this machine will lead to more pat-ents, and mine alone—I won't have to split the profits with anyone—and the more time I spend with this cobalt isotope, the more I'm seeing its possible adjacent applications, too."

"All right," she said. "Go on."

June is smart. I hadn't been telling her much about my work lately as she was so busy with Leora, but whenever I did, the questions she asked were engaged.

"Well, the idea for nuclear fission led me to the bomb, which led to this radiation machine, and I have a feeling that this machine will lead me back to the bomb. A different kind of bomb."

"I see."

I felt this need to prove myself to her. "I've been experi-menting with cobalt, and adding a neutron so that it becomes a radioactive isotope. When the pure cobalt becomes radio-active, my belief is that it will damage the genetic information in the cancerous cells and stop them from growing and spread-ing. It will be much more effective than surgery, because it can reach the cells that might escape a scalpel. I can target the radiation very specifically, like a laser beam, onto the affected area—the tumor. Probably fewer side effects than these new chemical therapy drugs, too."

"All right," she said. "And how will this translate to a different kind of bomb?"

"I'm still figuring that out, but based on my instincts and my initial research I believe that adding pure cobalt to a bomb would create the radioactive isotope upon detonation, and if the radiation is not hyper-targeted through beams, like with my machine, then it could propagate to form a nuclear explosion, with radioactive fallout, diffused, falling like dust. It would cause the genetic information in humans, and animals, and plants, to become altered, perhaps forever damaged. I can see a possibility of this bomb, if made large enough, killing every living thing on the planet."

"That sounds awful," she said.

"Truly. But every government would want one."

"And that," she went on, "would mean a lot of money."

"Yes, but it could never get made. I can't even tell anyone about it. The consequences of it would be far too great. Everything, June. Everything would be gone. What would be the point of any of this if it were all to disappear?"

"But what would happen if you patented it anyway? The nuclear chain reaction machine has the potential for great danger too, but you didn't have existential angst about patenting that, did you?"

"That was—that was a completely different situation. This is—"

"You wouldn't be doing anything wrong."

"Anything *wrong*?" I did not know her to be like this—so. . . immoral—so at first I had a hard time imagining what she could mean. "It's not the action itself that is wrong, it's the consequences."

"Well, the consequences wouldn't be your fault." She was speaking with the same neutral irreverence as if she were dissatisfied with my selection of wine.

She continued: "It's not like you to pass up an opportunity like this—it's *your* idea, so you deserve to get the money if it's developed."

I thought about what she was saying. "That's simply not right. If I file the patent, it will become public information. I can't let that happen."

"Who are you to say what is right or wrong?"

I had this feeling of dread building. "June. People cannot be trusted."

"You're being short-sighted. Nothing would *happen*, but this kind of money could completely change our lives."

"I can assure you that I have the full picture in mind, June. There would be no money unless it was developed, and this level of destruction would completely change—everything."

"Oh, you're always so dramatic."

"Do you understand me? I will never file this patent."

I could hear her tensing up, even through the phone lines. "I understand you, August."

Sometimes people speak more freely when they're not face-to-face, as they don't have to witness the reaction of their audience. June and I rarely spoke on the phone, and I wondered if this was what was happening. When had she become this . . . bitter? I wanted to ignore this conversation, and this new dark sharpness that was emerging from my wife.

"So you're just going to walk away from all this money," she said.

"You understand that this isn't about me, or you, or Leora, it's about global—"

"Oh of course I know, August," she said, interrupting me. "It was just a thought."

I paused, trying to shift gears back to the joy that had prompted me to make the call in the first place, simply wanting to spread that joy. *Just a thought.*

"Listen, Leora needs to use the potty," she said. "I have to go."

Then the line cut, and I felt quite alone.

I left the apartment with no place to go in mind. I walked until I found myself at the river, and then I followed the river to its mouth, to the lake. It was noon now, the sun high in the sky, the lake pummelled silver. There were cargo ships, pleasure boats, fishing boats. I never used the water as a thoroughfare and so forgot to consider it as such, but for many, it was a road like any other. For me, the water was the end, the point at which I could go no further.

There was a bench under a tree and when I saw it, I felt overcome with the need to sit. My heart was beating at such a pace. Joy sometimes feels just the same as sadness. I rested my head on my arms and watched shoes march on by—to my relief, their pace unslowed by my presence. Life goes on.

Leora might not remember me by the time I saw her again. Life goes on.

The war was raging in Europe, and still, life goes on. Birds make their nests, babies are born, lovers unite, tadpoles turn to frogs, people die. My insignificance is usually what calms me when I have these moments, but there, on that bench, it sat like an ice block on my heart.

Even now, here in this holding room, I will note that the ice has not melted. I have learned to live with it. Its presence is a reminder of what I have to do to keep going.

JUNE

It's becoming too claustrophobic in this tiny room, in my closed-up mind. To live fully in this state of limbo, in the moment right before the path forks, is exhausting. If I could sleep and turn off the thoughts for a while—but there's no point now.

Lately, when my daughter and I have been engaged in the typical parent-child standoffs, my resilience has vanished. When I tell her to do something and she says no, or if I say don't do something and she does it . . . I used to be able to weather some resistance, but now I want to scream, or smack her, do whatever it takes to *make her*. She is such a good girl almost all of the time, but a part of me cannot believe that her will exists separately to mine, and to be reminded of this causes intense, immediate rage. If I do scream (I've never smacked), then I am beset with an instant regret when met with her face: shock, dismay, betrayal. I can sense in these moments the fragility of her trust. If I did my worst and revealed this side of myself to her, she would accept it, which would be awful; in these moments, I can see that she would forget the mother she knew me to be and begin to live forevermore with this fine wire of fear in her heart.

Of course I love her, my daughter, my captor.

I take the biggest breath I can. I need a minute.

I wish I could just leave. Can I just—leave?

I check to make sure she's still asleep, her breath hot, her hands together in a prayer position under her cheek, and then I step outside the hotel room as if leaving my own head. The walls here in the corridor are the same mauve, the carpet the same flashy pattern. I slide down to sit on the floor, and just having a door behind my back makes things feel a little better. I try to take a breath deep enough to clean out my insides. I picture the air like a hand, scooping out the bottom of my lungs. I close my eyes for a moment, only to open them when I hear footsteps.

There's someone on their way down the hall. As the person gets closer, I can see it is a man, and he slows down when he sees me. As he approaches, I stand, and the man I'd assumed to be tall is revealed to be shorter than me. This shifts the power dynamic somewhat. I am a woman, alone, but I'm no longer as nervous now that I'm the one whose eyes look down upon him. His eyes, though, are like fireworks—the moment of light exploding.

"Evening," he says.

"Evening," I repeat.

He's holding his key, and he gestures to the door across from mine, as if to rationalize his having come so close. "It's quite late actually, isn't it—I suppose I should have said *morning*."

I am not wearing a watch. Time is nothing but inevitable. "Is it morning already?"

"Just past two o'clock." He nods. "Michael Harrop." He doesn't come to shake my hand and I can tell he is trying to keep his gaze slightly averted. It's late, we are alone in this hallway together, and his distance feels like a rather radical acknowledgement of his maleness.

"June," I say.

"Oh, my!—June?" he seems shocked. "June—Snow?"

"Have we . . . met?" I say, looking closely, suspiciously, at his face. His skin is tan, or olive, and there are lines where I imagine his smile would crease, into the cheeks, around the eyes. He has a neutral sort of look: unremarkable hair, unremarkable clothes. The kind of man who can blend into his surroundings. It's just the brightness of his green eyes that catches me off guard, but I know I have never seen them before. I'm good with faces.

"No, I'm sorry." He is suddenly speaking more quickly, energy animating his limbs. The way he looks at me has changed, too. I feel like a specimen. "I'm a journalist, I've been reporting on your husband's work for a long time, I know about you. I'm here to write about his trial. I thought you might be coming."

"Former husband," I say. While I know that August has been in the news I've never read any of it, so I've never considered the people who are writing about him. What they know. Whether it is different from what I know.

He swallows. "My apologies."

"You didn't know?"

He pauses. "I did know, but I didn't think it was public."

"You're thorough." I can feel him looking at me, assessing whether I am what he expected. This is the first person I have met in years who knows who I am, who knows my context. You know the feeling of standing in the wet sand as the waves lap your feet and the tide goes out, where you're slowly losing your footing, gradually sinking? That's how it feels.

"You're here to watch the trial?" he asks.

"I'm not here by coincidence."

He takes a step closer to me. The lights are immediately over his head now, and new shadows appear beneath his eyes. "Did you leave him after he filed the patent?" he speaks with this quiet, knowing tone, like he's trying to be a friend. I don't know what to say.

He continues: "You were together for years—did you know him to be capable of such devastation? Do you think he will try to plead innocence? Do you—"

"He never meant for this to happen," I interrupt. "I don't know how he will plead, but I do know he is innocent."

He pauses. "Innocent?" This man, this stranger, eyes me with confusion, even shock; I too am shocked. I wasn't expecting to say this. I didn't even know that I felt this. I didn't know it was possible to have secrets from one's own self. I wouldn't have thought I'd react this way: not fight, not flight, but truth.

If I am questioned tomorrow, I realize, then it will be the end of me. I have to leave now, or I will keep talking.

"I should get back to my daughter," I say, regretting instantly that he now knows she's here with me. My mind cycles through the possible ways in which this information could harm me or Leora and lands on nothing specific, which doesn't mean the anxiety leaves. In fact, it rises, with nothing to tether it down.

Without saying goodbye, I hurry back into my room. My back now on the other side of the door, I slump down onto the carpet and let my eyes adjust to the darkness. I can hear my blood pumping in my ears, and I can hear silence in the hall, which means that Michael Harrop must still be there, watching my door, thinking about what just happened, wondering how he will incorporate this news into his story, his angle.

"Mama?"

No, is my first thought. She was asleep—she is awake? "Leora?" I stand up.

"Where were you, Mama?" When I get to her I see that she is leaning with one arm on the bed, rubbing her eyes with the other hand. Her prosthetic is off and she does a single shuffle-hop towards me, using her arm to support her weight.

"You're awake? Darling." I go to her and crouch so we're the same height.

"You left."

"I just stepped outside for a second, sweetheart." Her baby hairs are stuck to her sleep-sweaty face. I stroke them up and away, reflexively.

"Were you talking to someone? I could hear your voice, and another voice. Was it Papa? Is he here?"

"Oh, yes—I mean, yes I was talking, but no, it's not your father. It was just—"

"Who was it?"

"It was, a cleaner, for the hotel."

"A cleaner?"

"Asking if we needed any towels."

"But we don't need any towels."

"You're right, that's just what I told the cleaner." I scoop her up, still my little girl, and sit down on her bed with her cradled in my lap.

"Is it morning?"

"Not yet, there's still lots of time for sleeping."

"Will you stay with me all the way until the morning?"

"Of course I will." I lay her down gently and sit on the mattress beside her. I always want to tuck her in even though she still always gets too hot. "I'm sorry I scared you, my darling."

"I didn't know where you were." Her face. She looks so sad and so relieved.

I remember the fear I had of her not needing me and I'm able to put it away cleanly, replacing it instead with the fear that she does need me, and that soon, I won't be there for her. I rub her back with my fingertips, whispering, "I'm right here, my baby, I'm right here," tears slipping through my closed eyelids.

AUGUST

The dust from the cobalt test bomb is diminishing, but its effects will continue for a long time yet. The layer of white encasing everything makes it all look so different.

When Leora first saw snow in the mountains of Denver she was too young to understand. For babies, everything, every day, is completely new; nothing is figured in as a constant. She was neutral to all variances, unable to create hierarchy among them. Bananas for breakfast one day, oatmeal the next. Only mother there one day, father also there the next. She didn't understand what a day was, or a flower, or a hand—hers or anyone else's. Weather was just an image through a window. But by the time she was two and winter returned, she could comprehend the change and it upset her. Change is difficult for children.

"Clean it up!" she said of the snow. "Turn it off!" She looked up to the sky, trying to see where it was coming from.

I could see in her face the shift when she realized that it was still the same world she loved underneath its new coating. Anger turned to surprise, delight. It was a world that had been translated, and she suddenly realized she could speak both languages.

I find solace in the natural world. I don't think June does. The deployment of my cobalt bomb would mean Leora would never get to see the world as I fell in love with it.

I can see the way to make things better and it isn't really so difficult, and yet I know it is impossible. When I was young, I thought everything was possible.

Science is a lineage of information, of one thing building upon the next, one idea leading to another, one invention standing on the shoulders of the one that came before it. In this way it reminds me a bit of springtime: how it always seems like a shock when the leaves and petals emerge from the dark ground and bare branches, even though we know they'd been a long time growing before they became visible.

I was always thinking of this inheritance in my work, but since with this project I was working alone, I considered all of the scientists who had paved the way for me—whether they were dead or alive—to be my colleagues. Émil Grubbé in Chicago had used x-rays to treat cancer with some success— he was perhaps the first. His first patient was a woman, called

Rose, just like my sister, suffering from inoperable cancer of the breast. But the rays did not cure her: she died of the cancer within a month. Grubbé was a homeopath and believed the rays to be a natural treatment, safe from the chemicals or toxins of drugs. He died due to exposure to all that radiation, just like Marie Curie died from her work.

There were more of them—many more—but for the purpose of streamlining, I edited the narrative as a novelist would and kept my characters to ones I felt I could control. It was just me, Émil, and Marie.

It was a year of working in this way after Leora's operation. Were it not for my staggering, impossible confidence—delusional, really, in the way that any true visionary must be—I would not have been able to pull it off.

The way that cobalt responded to radiation in my first experiment gave me the first seeds of faith that my machine would work. Cobalt was simple to produce, and the half-life was much longer than with radium, meaning, in simple terms, that this was a more stable element. Although describing it as "more stable" is perhaps rather philosophical. If something decays more slowly, we describe it as being less volatile, but this is relative and there are nuances within the term. Volatility is not inherent: it is manipulated. I digress. The cobalt exists for longer, and this was both safer and more convenient—the less decay, the fewer radioactive particles produced. I didn't want to die from this, as my departed fantasy colleagues had. Saving Leora's life should not occasion my own demise; I wasn't some *martyr*.

I had sketched out the machine and come up with a design that looked reasonable. It would work, I knew it would. It looked futuristic, almost like a rocket ship, and I hoped this modern feel would translate to the three-dimensional model, because I really did believe that this science-fiction appearance would help people to believe in it. All of the wires and tubes and jutting pipes of previous radiation machines looked to me more like torture devices, like how I had always imagined the one in Kafka's "In the Penal Colony," which I'd read of course in the original German. My machine would look clean, simple. Metal, light, lenses: almost like a telescope, except this would beam light instead of converging it. I asked the engineer at the university lab if I could hire him to build it for me, as I wasn't about to teach myself all that.

It took him ten weeks to construct, and when I saw it, gleaming in the dark, it really did take my breath away. It's the closest I've ever come to feeling like an artist, and the power this made me feel was even greater than I would have expected.

A year of living underwater, and then, finally coming up for air.

Shortly after I first saw my machine, I learned that that Antonio had been awarded, himself alone, the Nobel Prize in Physics for inducing radioactivity by neutron bombardment. The experiment I had come up with. *My* idea. A million dollars. They called him "the architect of the nuclear age," and this was the beginning of the slow erasure of my name from all of the future's history books.

The bed in this room has a grey woollen blanket with a blue stripe around its perimeter. The wool is surprisingly soft but the mattress is stiff, hard as the floor, thus sacrificing the opportunity for comfort. I move from the bed to the window and close my eyes. I try to picture a place where I felt happy.

I can see the wind blowing across the lake, dimpling the water, pine trees sticking up along the shore like paintbrushes all in a row. In my mind's eye, my mother is behind me, cooking dinner. My brother and sister were probably playing by the fire, or in the woods with our father. I am standing at the window of the lovely little cottage on Lake Balaton that we visited in the summers when I was a child. Nobody is paying attention to me, or that's how it felt, and I feel joy in one of the rare privacies afforded in childhood.

Sometimes, when I feel myself under stress, I try to imagine myself in a movie and decide what music would be playing for the viewer, underscoring my emotional state. It's an exercise in detachment, or detached attachment; I'm not sure which it is, but it makes me feel better. I compose the song in my mind, not for myself but for my imaginary audience. I said I don't make music anymore, but if you count this—well, I suppose you wouldn't.

The music I imagine playing as the soundtrack to this memory—though in fact, I know that there was only silence, as my mother liked quiet in the evenings after spending the whole day with her noisy children—is something beautiful but chaotic, something anachronistic to my childhood but resonant with the present. Dizzy Gillespie, maybe, with his abstracted improvisation and flatted fifths making the melody feel dissonant, disorienting, but all the more captivating. Like a story you have to know the end of.

As we were lying in bed one night, in the long and blurry years before Leora arrived and changed the way that time flowed, June asked me to do this exercise. To close my eyes and imagine a place where I felt happy. We were in our tiny room in London, caught between waves of uncertainty and rising tides of war, not sure how long we would be there or where we might go next, or what we would do for money when the savings ran out, and I followed her instructions. I could see the candlelight through my closed eyelids, I could feel the warmth of her soft body next to me in bed.

"Where are you thinking about?" she asked after a few moments of silence.

"Here," I said. "Right now. Just lying in bed with you, evening, candles. I'm happy here."

When we love something, we give it value. Things have no inherent value without our loving them. It appears as though *this*—chaos, destruction, and death—is what I have loved. And this breaks my heart. I love the world, all of it, everyone and everything on this planet, and the all-consuming, generalized nature of my love means that of course I will love destruction too, for it is part of life; and of course I will love those who have evil in them, for they are as human as I am; and of course I will love death, because what reasonable man can fear the inevitable?

JUNE

I wasn't a perfect wife. I wasn't even a good wife, much of the time. I cheated on him (oh, of course I haven't told you that), and lied to him about it. I disagreed with him on so many things, and disobeyed him every time I brought Leora to synagogue. I wrote letters on his behalf, forging his signature. Sometimes he asked me to do this, and other times, he most definitely did not. I kept acting out, like a child, desperate for his attention. But is that love? Or despair?

The first year of Leora's remission was a year of turning away from the grief that I am only fully facing now, in the midst of all of this. It was the year of feeling only marginally within the limits of normality, knowing that the whole time a hawk was circling me, its prey, vigilant for the moment I might let my tiny mouse-heart slip out from where I kept it in my throat.

The way I saw the world when I was with her was almost as if everything was in translation—a slightly different version of itself—but rather than, as before, making me feel fogged and detached, this now made me see things with such a sharp clarity. To give an explanation of something that would make sense to her forced me to examine it anew. And how good it made me feel to see things as new.

A lemon once went mouldy in the fruit bowl and when Leora asked why I had thrown it in the garbage, I told her, without much thought, that it was because "the lemon has gone bad." Every time she saw a lemon after that, for months, she would ask, in a nervous whisper, "Mama, did this lemon do bad things?" In her mind, actions had consequences, and the lemon was being punished for a crime it had committed.

As Leora gained a greater understanding of her world, she started asking questions, naturally, about her leg.

One night at bedtime, when I was lying beside her in her twin bed as she drifted in her soft, cuddly pre-sleep, she asked me, for the first time, "Mama, where did my leg go?" She knew it was gone—she was asking *where* it had gone.

I wished I knew what to tell her that would make her not afraid. I didn't care what the truth was. I couldn't handle knowing if her leg had been burned or thrown out in the medical waste. Anything I could think to say along these lines was awful. It would terrify her. In my silence, she started forming her own thoughts.

"Did my leg . . . go for a walk?"

"Yes," I said, with relief so enormous it was just like joy, "that's exactly where it went. It went for a walk to see the world."

She had come up with her own answer that fit into the logic of her worldview. This made her happy, and not afraid, and she had done it on her own. Sometimes she would ask, while eating a snack, her eyes all lit up, "Mama, where is my leg now?"

And we'd make up stories together about her leg on a beach in California, or hopping on a bus on the way to school, going to learn about all sorts of interesting things.

After a few months of adapting to life with a single set of toes, a single ankle, a single calf, and a single knee, and after the swelling had gone down, and after the wounds had healed, I took Leora to get fitted for her first prosthetic. It was only the first, as it would need to be replaced every year until she was five, during those years of rapid growth, and then every two years after that until she was fully grown. In my mind, this made it sort of just a practice run. She could use it if she wanted, or not. I didn't like the idea of her body not being her own—it seemed too close to the way I'd felt about the cancer invading her body.

"New leg day!" I said that morning when I went to wake her up, earlier than normal. That's what I'd been calling it. I'd set it up for her as if the doctors were working with sculptors to create a special present for her. She was excited. She was excited about most things.

We arrived at the meeting with the physiotherapist and the leg was on the floor in the middle of the room. She was sitting in her pram, and she leaned back into it, rather than reaching out her arms for me to help her get out. That it was bulky, not lean like her own, and the smooth plastic a pallid, lifeless colour, dulled Leora's enthusiasm. She wanted to give every one of her toys a name—sometimes insisting on naming carrot sticks, individual wooden blocks, a beautiful white flower—and when I saw that leg, I hoped she wouldn't want to name it. My instinct was that it would be ideal for her to come to consider it part of her body, not something separate. What did I know, though? It was her leg, it was her body.

"We'll dress it up," I told her, as she slowly reached up to clutch my hand. "It will wear socks and tights just like the other leg. It will become your leg." She looked up at me, shiny eyes, as the leg lay there like a dead thing.

The physiotherapist fitted the plastic lump to Leora's half-leg stump with straps that went around her hips. It was a bit big for her, and she stumbled. She looked up at me again and I could see the worry in her face: the downturn of her eyebrows, the instant dip of the sides of her mouth. I could tell she was not just uncomfortable, but she was, for some reason, afraid of displeasing me, and my heart broke in yet another new way. I tried to smile encouragingly through the swell of emotion.

"Look at you!" I said. "You're doing it!"

Leora looked down at the stiff lump of the foot at the base of her new attachment, and tried again to take a step. The knee did not articulate as a human's does, and was more rigid than a child's, certainly — kneecaps don't even develop until age three, and here was a giant plastic ball upon which the calf bone rotated only front to back. This time, she fell down.

I hurried across the room, four quick and unfairly easy steps, to scoop her up before the tears spilled over the ledges of her lower lids.

"You're okay," I said, rocking her back and forth on the floor. "You're okay. Let's take this off for now," I looked up at the physiotherapist, motioning for help in removing it. "You did great, sweetheart."

"Thank you, sweetheart," Leora said back to me.

"With practice, she'll get used to it," the woman said, in a tone I found patronizing, as if she were implying that this fake leg was better than nothing. Of course it was. But what would have been better still would be her own leg, never taken.

What I'm trying to say is that it had taken me that full year of Leora's life — from eighteen months to two and a half years old — to let myself love my daughter again with my whole heart, without holding back for fear of losing her. I had finally gotten there. I could hold her without crying. I could sing her lullabies without having to stop to hide the sobs. I could sleep through the night, some nights, without nightmares.

And then, less than two weeks after the fitting, at a checkup exactly one year after her amputation, the doctors told me that she had relapsed. The cancer was here again. Leora was there with me. The doctors didn't speak to me privately ahead of time, clearly thinking she was young enough to not understand anything, and this mistake of theirs allowed me to feel anger before I felt any of the other feelings.

"The X-ray shows a small lump has returned," her primary doctor said.

I repeated his sentence in my mind. I separated all the words. *Small* meant nothing; size was irrelevant. She was small, and her predator was back. I focused on the word *returned*. As if it were a house guest that had come back to stay a while longer. As if a return was inevitable. I tried to swallow but couldn't get any liquid down. My insides had frozen over.

"What's happening, Mama?" Leora at my side, her warm body, her legs dangling off the examination table.

She always asked what was happening when I read her a story, even in the books that we read constantly. She sensed, or remembered, when tension was rising. I could see how uncertainty made her uncomfortable. *What's happening? What's going to happen? Is that the butterfly? Is the bunny sad?* She wanted the reassurance of structure even though she knew the form.

What to tell her, in that moment? How could I explain what was happening in her body, or in my mind? How to tell her that she had to go through this again and I had no fight left in me? Survival was less likely after relapse. I knew this in my doctor-brain but denied the fact entrance into my mother-heart. I had never used the word *death* around her, never mentioned things as dying or dead, having chosen to shield her—why? for whom?—from things like flowers browning or worms that stopped moving. Instead I reframed, or outright lied. The flowers will come back next year, I'd say. The worm is having a rest.

August had told me that this day might be coming, but I'd refused to believe in that possibility. I had to believe that she would be fine, safe, in order to be able to live. I needed to live as if we were free. And now that the day had finally come, I had no defences.

If it had been me, I would have given up. But it was my daughter, not yet three, full of love and questions, full of my whole heart, and so I was unable to bury myself. I wanted to disappear, to cease existence, but I could not.

I hugged her, and smiled. To answer her question, I said, looking at the doctor: "The doctor saw a little lump in your leg, and your daddy is going to take it away. Everything will be fine."

"Daddy will?"

"Yes. Daddy's machine will take it away."

"Is everything fine . . . right now?"

"Yes, my love. Now we will go home and make some dinner. Everything is fine."

I sent a telegram that night. *It's back.*

The next morning, he called.

"June? You're awake. How is she?"

"August." We were always up early. "She doesn't seem to be in pain like last time, it wasn't sore or anything."

"What's she doing now?"

It was so good to hear his voice.

"She's sitting here watching me. Hi, love. Do you want to tell Daddy about your new leg?"

"I have a new leg," she shouted from the floor.

"She still hasn't worn it, though," I hushed into the mouthpiece, then said louder: "Say it into the phone, sweetheart." I put the receiver to her ear and she froze like she always did when asked to perform on command, and smiled instead of speaking. The thought of her no longer being here, smiling or speaking. I couldn't. I had carried this thought with me for a year and it had finally gone to sleep, only to be awoken again.

"Hi," she said. "Hi, Daddy." Then off she shuffled to pull some bowls out of drawers.

When I brought the receiver back to my ear August was still speaking to her, describing a fluffy white dog he had seen on his walk that morning.

"It's me again," I said. "The dog sounds nice."

And then for a few moments we just stayed there, far apart, breathing together. I tried to picture what his view might be like, what he'd be seeing right then as we stood, together but separately, but it had been too long since I'd been there to remember.

"I have a prototype. It's ready for Leora. I will fly you both out here, and we'll use it on her."

"It's done?" I hadn't realized it was so close.

"It's going to work, June. I know it will."

So that was it. His work had been progressing. The machine was ready. I was just as relieved that my line to Leora wasn't a complete fabrication as I was that this might actually work.

AUGUST

The sky is beginning to remember what light is. It is still black, but a hopeful shade of black, rather than completely obscure. The cockroach is beginning to wake up and shake open its wings. I can see the outlines of trees again, demarcating dark from darker. My face is hovering, disembodied above my dark grey shirt, in the window that has once again become mirrored as the balance of light has tipped.

I used to be rather handsome, though I didn't think so at the time. Seeing old photographs—my passports, university identity cards—I can see now what I could not then. I looked distinguished, perhaps even noble, but certainly optimistic. My eyes were so open. There was a symmetry to my face that time has taken away.

I am aware of my vanity only in that I feel a sense of sadness that the people whom I meet now have no awareness that

I was once a sharp young man. I know from having once been young myself that when people see a fat old man, they see only a fat old man. I am a frumpy foreigner, fallen from grace, and I belong nowhere. I once felt myself, with my precarious but portable life, at home in any place, and now I feel like a refugee in my whole existence: a European exiled from Europe, a physicist exiled from physics, a father exiled from his family. My life is small, and getting smaller.

In the spring of 1943, when Leora's cancer was back, I was ready. I booked June and Leora on the flight to Chicago the day after I spoke with them, and spent the rest of the afternoon pacing, preparing. I looked around my small apartment and felt nervous, seeing it through their eyes. I had no toys for Leora, let alone a place for her to sleep. Could a three-year-old—or no, she wasn't quite three yet—sleep on the couch? I didn't know what foods she liked. I knew I should go to the shops to fill the fridge and cupboards, but I didn't know where to begin.

When they arrived, it felt like there were too many people in the space. I didn't feel at home with them there, at home in my own body. I don't know how else to explain it. Their stuff was everywhere. Leora didn't sit still. The way she moved without her leg seemed already to be seamless, comfortable. She didn't seem to miss anything. June had brought the prosthetic, but Leora didn't like using it. Just as she'd held herself up using chairs and tables when she was learning to stand, she seamlessly maneuvered herself around the room by moving from one piece of furniture to the next, and if there was an expanse of floor with no handles to help her, she shuffled on her bum to the bookshelf or the windowsill to pull herself up to examine what had caught her eye. She was different, and she was the same.

"Daddy!" she cried out with delight every few minutes, as if she had forgotten where she was for a moment and then suddenly remembered. "Daddy's window!" She smacked her hands on the wooden sill, looking up and down and side to side, confronted with the darkness of the brick wall facing the window in my tiny kitchen. "Daddy, where's sky? Where's sky?"

I walked over to her and sat beside her, this bright thing, and I looked over to June, sitting on the couch in her own world. "Well," I said to my daughter, "just because you can't see something doesn't mean it isn't there."

June wasn't looking at me. She'd hardly even spoken since they'd arrived. I couldn't tell if she was nervous, or angry, or something else. I kept picturing some man, an affair, as the ghost between us, the reason for our divide, but I see now that if there was a ghost it was only me: it was the shape of who I should have been.

On the day of the experiment, Leora was on the table underneath the metal oculus of my machine. She had to be sedated so that she wouldn't move. The rays from the cobalt must be aimed at the precise location of the tumor; even the calmest of toddlers would wriggle and fidget and disorient the invisible beam. The anesthesiologist was at the side of the narrow table on which Leora lay; June was at the other side. She'd wanted to stroke her face until she fell asleep. It was such a tender picture. I had never seen June put Leora to bed, but there must have been this same kind of scene every day, which broke my heart a little bit.

I turned to the technician who had been trained to operate the machine. "Charlie? Are you ready?"

Charlie was a young man, fresh out of college, who had been part of the meetings in which I had briefed the hospital staff, and he had been very upfront in voicing his concerns. He was worried, as my wife was, that this new technology was too risky to use on anyone. He questioned my ethics in wanting to use it on my own child. I didn't take offense to this, for I understood where he was coming from. He still had that slightly rebellious confidence of a student, challenging authority, and I admired him for it, but I flipped the argument: how could I *not* use everything in my arsenal to try to save my own child?

"But it could be better to do nothing, couldn't it?" he had said. "Especially if doing something could mean it might kill her?"

"But doing nothing will definitely kill her."

Now Charlie responded, uneasy but unwavering, "Yes."

Everyone was in their places. The lights were dimmed, the machine was gleaming. I had a familiar feeling of weightlessness, a feeling of flying. I suppose this is what hope feels like. With a certainty as deep as my bones, I knew that the technology would work, that it would save lives, that it would change the world. With this feeling came—"pride" is too simple a word. It's more like I felt, finally, *worthy*.

"All right," I said to Charlie. "Flip the switch at my signal."

June left our sleeping child and came with me into the hallway. We stood beside each other by the large viewing window. I made eye contact with Charlie, and nodded. He approached my daughter, and the Cobalt-60 machine, and double-checked the positioning of everything. He looked back at me, gave a firm nod, and then went to the wall where the switch was.

"Are you worried?" June asked.

"No," I lied.

She looked at me. I could tell that she knew I was lying, but that she was grateful for it. "If this works, then—"

"I know."

The beam only needed to be illuminated for a few seconds. This one was probably finished already. The sedation would last an hour, though, so I waited, and watched, though I knew nothing would be revealed for many days.

Then June interrupted the silence: "How's the cobalt bomb going?"

"Nowhere." I was surprised by the question—it seemed so out of place to me then. "I'm focused on treating Leora."

"I thought one thing led to another."

"You know where my priorities are," I said, but perhaps, in fact, she did not. Perhaps she doubted me. Or maybe I had not clearly communicated my intentions, my . . . entire identity.

By this point in my life I had stopped thinking of myself and others in terms of the boat and the island, like my mother had told me. I was not distracted by the unknowability of others; I accepted it, and didn't try to cross the distance in order to understand. That was my mistake. I didn't see, or appreciate, June's hunger, her dissatisfaction. I knew that I'd angered her during that phone call several months ago, when I told her I would not patent the cobalt bomb technology. She had always told me she wanted more from me—more of my time, and if not that, then more of my money. There was nothing more to it than that. "Selfish" isn't the right word—she had a need, and I dismissed her. I was annoyed, not even giving her the boldness of my anger in return. I felt as though I was the keeper of this knowledge and that it was my job to protect the world from it. What ego! Knowledge cannot be contained, I know that now. It was condescending of me to believe that June would listen to me simply because I thought she *should*, the same way a child is supposed to listen to their parents. And so, you see, this was not her fault.

When I found out, I wasn't upset with her, no. I was terrified for us all.

JUNE

As she lay there on the gurney, the sedation kicking in, I explained to Leora that her father had built her this machine to get rid of the lump in her leg.

"It will make me feel better?" she said.

She wasn't feeling sick, which was confusing for her. There was no pain like last time, and the cancer was causing no secondary symptoms.

"There is a light inside of the machine Daddy built for you, and it will take away the lump here," I stroked her knee.

"Will the light make my leg come back?"

"No, my love." I was about to say that it would mean instead that she might not have to lose any more of her leg, or the other leg, or any other part of her body. I was about to say that it would, we hoped, stop her from dying. But then I remembered that this was my child, my baby; she wasn't a grown-up, not a patient of mine, and I couldn't explain nuance, or risk, or my fears. I was allowed to say nothing.

August and I watched Leora through a window into the procedure room. We held hands. I closed my eyes. I saw my father as he looked when I was little. I saw blue, the dark blue ocean with yellow light filtering through all the particles; I remembered swimming in the Mediterranean when I was a child and in the Pacific on that trip to Vancouver with August, and what it felt like to be surrounded by the silence and majesty of the deep unknown. I saw the blue of the mountains in the morning from my childhood bedroom window, a dusky cloak of periwinkle covering the entirety of the rock, backlit by apricot skies. I saw the blue of Leora's eyes when she first woke up from her newborn sleep, but the blue of them felt like a recognition, like a reunion with a soulmate I'd known all my life but had never met before. Back then they were the blue of a glacial pool in the mountains, but they've since become a deeper blue, sometimes a grey or even almost-black, like the colour of the night sky just as it's becoming morning.

August and I stood there, side by side each day, for ten days, holding hands for those five minutes, and it was the closest I've felt to him in a long time; perhaps ever. Our marriage was not one where we could read each other's thoughts or finish each other's sentences. I never knew what his glances or sighs meant. In some ways it was a blessing to have this

distance, to always think of the other as not entirely know-
able. Even if you believe it at times to be otherwise, you really
can never know anyone else. Now I was standing beside him,
watching our daughter alongside him, and we were seeing the
same thing, through the same window. This was literal and
also carried the weight of metaphor.

Leora had to lie in the exact same spot on the table every
day, with the radiation—it was completely invisible—beam-
ing onto her leg in the exact same place (marked with ink on
her skin to be sure) for all ten days. Each session only took a
few minutes, and all she had to do was lie there. The sedation
made her limp and foggy for the rest of the day.

At the end of the ten days, the night before Leora and I
were about to fly home again, leaving August behind, he and
I had the same fight we always had. I wanted to be close to
him, he wanted his freedom. The closeness we had had during
her treatment made me realize that it was possible. I could see
what I had been missing.

"What you expect of me is more than anyone can expect of
a wife," I said, hours into the argument, finally seeing within
myself a truth I'd never expressed before. It felt like there was
a beam of light, illuminating what I felt.

"But I have *no* expectations of you," he said. "I've let you
live your life however you wanted."

"That's not true," I shouted from the dark bedroom in his
tiny apartment, not thinking of our sleeping daughter on the

couch—the *couch*—beyond the closed door, in the living room, "that's not true at all. I had to live my life according to the rules that *you* set up, I had to work around the situations that you arranged for yourself. And I wanted you to have expectations of me! Of course I did! I *wanted* you to want me to be a good wife and a good mother! I *wanted* you to want me *with* you! To want me all to yourself!" I took a breath. "Everything I did, I did as a reaction to you."

How sad it seemed, framed that way.

"And a marriage," I continued, since he didn't seem about to take a turn to speak, "is about expectations. This is not a marriage. This is an affair you've been having with your wife for fourteen years."

This is when I stopped loving him. It happened in a moment. Or, at least, I realized it in a single moment, which is a sign, I suppose, that it had been happening all along, the inevitable result of years of bitterness and neglect, but it felt as sudden and complete as the collective silencing of birds immediately before a storm. When he reached out to touch me I felt my skin recoil. This frightened me. I was no longer attached to him, to anything. I had thought all along that his love would destroy me, and I was happy to surrender myself to the crush of it. I believed it was worth it. But in the end, it was not destruction, it was release.

All along, August had been looking through a different window. When he watched Leora undergo her radiation treatment, he saw how much work still needed to be done:

on the machine, on perfecting it, on distributing it, on understanding the nature of the cobalt, and what happened when it became ionized.

When I watched her, I saw our daughter, this product of the love my husband and I had, and I saw her at the end, hopefully, of this period of sickness, and at the beginning of a period of calm for us all. I thought the intensity of August's work would be over, and that our life as a family could finally begin. I was wrong.

For ten days I sat with Leora as she was sedated, and then watched from the window with August as an invisible force worked upon her. After those ten days, Leora and I went home. August walked us to the cab, which would take us to the airport, and kissed each of us on the cheek.

And that was the last time I saw him. Of course, I didn't know it would be the last. We never know the end of something as it's happening. It's only in the aftermath that we create a narrative, and story can only ever be a cousin of truth.

One way of defining who you are is who you are *not*, and I had spent so much time considering the ways in which August was absent from me, the ways in which his ambition equalled my passivity and his detachment created my desiring, that I had stopped wondering who I was alone, separate. I had worried that if our marriage broke, all that would be left was a broken thing, and shards of a broken bowl serve no purpose.

When our marriage fell apart and I did not die, as I had feared I might, I felt lighter, and more powerful, than I could have imagined. I was no longer a bowl, but I had never been a bowl, and no longer even had any need for bowls. Do you know what I mean? Is this what freedom is? I had nothing to be afraid of anymore.

AUGUST

I am August. I worked so hard. And I did it: I saved my daughter.

JUNE

I have the feeling that time is running out and I have not yet gotten to the end of my story. Night is becoming day. Soon we will have to leave this room and walk into our futures. Though for many days over the past five years I have craved independence, I would happily stay here, linked with Leora, and stop time forever. Look at her. She's so perfect. Why did I never think this was enough?

I suppose it's obvious that I wouldn't be feeling so anxious about tomorrow if I were completely uninvolved, completely blameless. I haven't been able to even say it out loud to myself. I can't even get near the idea that I will be separated from Leora. Would she be taken away from me right there, in the courtroom? She would be so scared. I can see her face exactly, the way her worried eyebrows make an arch across her forehead. I've kissed her every single day of her life. I know every particle of food that she has consumed, ever. These aren't the things I would miss, but they are the things that have made up my days, my years. I don't know, exactly, what I would miss. Just, her. And—I hope this doesn't sound wrong, given the circumstances—but I would miss the precise moment, right after she has gone to sleep, when I have the whole evening to myself after having been entertaining her and negotiating with her all day, and I feel the tug of love, the feeling of *missing* her. I would miss missing her, because I would miss her all the time.

Before I get into the details, please remember: though this might seem like a monumental betrayal, August had betrayed me so many times that the feeling had become a texture, woven into the fabric of our dynamic.

August had told me how much the cobalt bomb could be worth if developed, and he still wouldn't patent it despite my urging, so when we got home from the radiation treatment, I registered for a patent using his name. I sent off for the paperwork, and it was me who filed it with the United States Patent Office. I had been doing his paperwork for years—I knew the vernacular.

The envelope arrived in the mail on a gloomy, drawn-out autumn morning when Leora was having a nap. I wasn't sure if she was still tired from the effects of the treatment, but she was sleeping more than usual. I knew as soon as I saw the postman what it was. I could feel that heaviness in the air. I opened the brown package more carefully than I normally open my mail, and felt the precipice of a before-and-after moment.

But I know that this narrative of receiving the approval being the transformative moment is false. It's impossible to pin down one event in the whole series of small actions that lead to monumental moments. We do this only to make sense of our lives. Did this whole thing begin, in fact, with meeting August? Did a seed get planted the first time I felt a distance between us? You know what I mean.

I didn't feel at all guilty when I filed the papers. I was so angry at him that it eliminated my sense of scale. It felt like my actions were exclusively between myself and August, not between the world and me. I wanted to punish him, to make him hurt. I wanted to *win*.

When the cheques rolled in, I realized that August was right, he was always right: the human appetite for destruction will outweigh our desire for life, and a terror dawned on me.

We've earned almost eight hundred thousand dollars so far, and it's only been a year and a half since the patent was approved. Over the next eighteen years, until the patent expires, we will likely receive millions.

August is not on trial for having this idea; he's on trial for formalizing it. For stoking fears, and profiting from the inevitable. He is on trial for my actions. He has every right to tell the truth tomorrow, and I have spent all this time wondering whether or not he is the type of man who will. It's disorienting to not know. It feels wrong, even shameful, that I could not be certain about this, after all these years—like I wasted my time getting to know him. I don't think that's the case, exactly, but I am of two minds: he is a man who values truth in its biggest-picture sense; and he is also a man who believes in the grey area, though it frustrates him. He is pecuniary-minded, he is fearful, he is vain. He is noble, he is ambitious, he has such a love for the world that he is always left disappointed. If I knew whether or not he still loved me, I might be able to predict.

When Leora was first born, in those dark months I lived only in my head, I would hold her and rock endlessly in the glider I'd moved to the window, so that at least I could see something of the world I wasn't able to participate in. I held her warm body, this tiny baby who knew nothing of anything, and I'd watch the weather come, and the day pass. As I held her, my baby who didn't yet know what a thought was, who only existed in the present tense and was content so long as her needs were met, I just couldn't bear that I had brought this perfect creature into the world and that she too would know sadness. It felt like I was holding a bomb.

How could I be guilty? I only wanted to make sure that August was paid for his work. A person can be guilty for an idea, this I understand, but can I be guilty for bringing the idea into the world? Can I be guilty for making sure that Leora had a good life?

If people think we are guilty, they think it is the money that makes us guilty. Us—me, or him.

If he speaks against me tomorrow, he could get Leora back. She is still young enough to fall in love with him all over again—and what will become of me?

III

JUNE

It's nearly time to wake Leora. I can see her living out something in her dreams, some kind of story, but I will never know what it is. It's impossible to tell whether she's happy or sad or scared or, like August usually said of his dreams, simply living out banal recreations of the days. Leora never remembers her dreams. I don't think she's yet able to distinguish dream from memory, just as it's sometimes tricky for her to separate pretending from lying. How to explain to a child that a fairy tale isn't a lie, but a story? Or that memory, even if she doesn't remember it, is truth, not fiction?

She thinks she will be able to hug her father tomorrow—today. That they will be spending the day together. The anticipation of this is so real in her mind that I wonder whether the vision alone, which has lasted for many days now, is strong enough to transform into memory, superseding the truth. For her sake, I hope so. The fiction will be better than the fact.

The public will love August more than me. They already do—it would be impossible for them not to. I fell in love with his ideals too—with that sad, passionate hope of his. Everyone does. His accomplishments are the mark of a great man. And he's consumed so much of their attention; even if he's been portrayed, by some, as the "bad guy," he is still the main character. Even my neighbour Nick, I'd bet, would be happy if August were set free. Whether or not he really believes in his innocence, such an ending would satisfy Nick's sense that this is a man who has always known what he was doing, who has been creating the narrative all along.

In front of the court, in front of the whole world, August will tell his people that he never meant to do any harm, and they will see that, for it is the truth. When he starts talking about the motivations behind his initial research they will be captivated, I'm sure, even if they can't quite follow. Everyone is. He has a way about him. They will think of him as a good man.

What they won't see are ways that he abandoned me. How he turned me to this. Even if they did see all that, it wouldn't matter. They might pity me, they might scorn me, but they will definitely judge me. Regardless of whether or not August tells the whole story tomorrow, regardless of whether or not he is proclaimed guilty, he will be beloved. He will be the favourite, for his story is larger than mine. You don't even see the way that my story is a microcosm of the same thing. Of life, of creation, of power. How I, too, triumphed over death. August saved her life, and just like a firefighter rescuing a child from a burning building, he will be the one people talk about. Not the mother, who gave life in the first place. The mother is as inevitable as a puddle after the rain. History is written by the victors and inherited by the losers, not the mothers.

I shower, even though I had a bath just a few hours ago. I want to cling to the routine of it all. I dress myself in the freshly pressed outfit I spent so long deliberating over. I carefully put on my makeup, feeling the flesh of my face slip over the bones beneath as I smooth out the paint that matches the colour of my skin.

I never thought August and I would reunite after our separation, but I also realize, for the first time, that I never thought that possibility would be . . . impossible. And now it will be. Add this to my cocktail of sadness.

I sit on Leora's bed now and watch her perfect face. Now that she is five, I miss when she was four; when she was four, I missed when she was three. Her growth has been a marker for the passage of time since we last saw August. The last time he saw her, she didn't know the word "constellations," or know how to identify any of them, or speak French, or know how to braid her own hair (not well, but still). The last time he saw her, she hadn't mastered the use of her prosthesis and, at almost three years old, preferred still to be carried, or pushed in her pram. At five, I only carry her if she's fallen asleep in my bed and I have to move her to her own. She doesn't fully wake up, but she does wrap her arms around me and nuzzle into the crook of my neck. I love that moment. I walk slowly, and hold her for as long as I can. One of my few early memories of my mother is of her carrying me while I slept, or pretended to. I remember wanting to pretend to be asleep so that she would not make me walk. I loved to be sleepy and carried but was *such a big girl*, I would never have *let* her carry me. The carrying had to be a secret, passive surrender. Mothers are good at this. At knowing the distinction. At going along with it. We intuit, we observe the unspoken, we do the invisible work and remain invisible.

He writes her letters, still. He is a good father. We both pretend that I am not the one who has to read the letters out loud to her, and that they are not full of messages for me, too.

He writes about things he sees on his walks, dogs and funny hats, and what he eats for breakfast. He will send a postcard if he goes anywhere, and describe what it looks like from his window. He always asks questions, though we never write back. What did you do today? Have you learned any new jokes? Have you ever eaten a snail? (She laughed so hard at that one. "Snails are not for eating!") In all of the letters, he never mentioned the trial.

Sitting by her side, my weight shifting her position in the bed, Leora starts to sense my presence. I stroke her face with my fingertips, and her legs—I still call them legs, plural—start to stretch out like they did when she was a baby, like I could even feel when she was still inside of me.

"Mama?" she opens her eyes.

"Good morning, my love."

"Is Daddy here?"

"No, darling, we have to get you dressed and fed and then we will go to the room where Daddy will be."

Getting dressed is often a fight with her but today she does it quickly, all by herself. I order room service and she eats everything, again with no argument.

She leaves the rinds of the oranges, the crusts of the toast. The shell of her hard-boiled egg looks like the aftermath of an explosion. She looks at the breakfast graveyard thoughtfully. "Can we go see Daddy now?"

I want to protect her from what will come next, but I can't.

When I was pregnant, I developed a deep fear that the birth would kill me. I researched all I could about maternal health statistics and prenatal care. I wasn't worried about Leora. I could feel her strength inside of me. But this is when my terror of leaving her began. Time gradually brought me further from the post-natal depression I experienced after her birth, but now, in this long, stretching limbo, I feel closer to that fear than I have in years. I am again living within uncertainty, and the familiarity of this feeling awakens a world of memories, suddenly so present I could walk right into them, inhabit them fully.

"Daddy might not be able to play with you today, Leora. We will probably be able to wave, and say hello, but he will have to sit far apart from us today."

"What about later?" she asks. "We will be able to play later, right?"

She's always had this optimism. Sometimes it's felt more like stubbornness.

"Maybe, darling. I'm not sure."

"I think we will."

I've been conscious ever since she was very young of using the language of ambivalence with her. I'm not sure why this was important to me, but I wanted her to know that I didn't know everything, that certain things were altogether unknowable, that facts were sometimes slippery and changeable. If she pointed to a picture of a cat and said it was a tiger, I'd merely say, "It looks like a cat to me." I'd never tell her that she was wrong and I was right. If she asked what a certain flower was, even if I was quite sure, I'd say, "I think that is a tulip." Being a parent can be so authoritarian. Uncertainty seemed to bring with it more humility. I can see now that this has translated within her to this spark of hopefulness I find so heartbreaking. I won't tell her something definitively won't happen, and so she finds hope within the possibility.

"I need to tell you, Leora"—it is time to prepare her—"that when we see Daddy, people will be asking him questions about what happened a long time ago. The people think he might have done something bad."

"I don't think he's done something bad," she says.

"Your Daddy loves you and would never do anything bad to you. But from his work, his science, something bad has come. And today the people have to decide whether he is bad because of this bad thing."

She looks offended. "My Daddy is not bad."

I had planned to tell her that I was also involved in the bad thing, and that her Daddy knew, but nobody else did, and that I was scared that soon they might find out. It felt wrong to keep this from her; it felt important to be honest. She is—well, though I know she's only five, sometimes, she feels like my best friend. Mainly, I don't want it to come as a surprise.

I open my mouth to try to explain this, but I can't. And then I realize: I don't have to. I don't know why I've thought I need to treat her like an adult, like an equal. She is five! Telling her would do nothing but confuse and frighten her. I don't want to make her have to experience the fear twice— the fear that something might also happen to me, and then the fear because it *was* happening. Better just once.

"What's going to happen to him if the people think he's bad?"

"Well, if that happens, we might not see him for a while, but we haven't seen him in a long time already, and we've been fine, haven't we? Even if we can't see him, he will still write letters."

"And if he's not bad, will he come home with us?"

"His home is a different home, remember? Daddy's home is not in England."

"Maybe he will come home later," she says. "What are you doing, Mama?"

She takes my hand down from my forehead. I hadn't realized I was pulling out my eyebrow hairs with my fingers.

"Oh, I'm sorry, sweetheart."

I try to think of something to say that might calm the friend in my head, to make her feel better, but I can't think of anything. I close my eyes for a moment, grip my hands together so they can't keep up with their idle destruction of my face, and take a deep breath. *Whatever happens, will happen*, I say to my friend. *There's nothing you can do now.*

"Open your eyes, Mother, I want to go now." She takes my hand, and we walk out of the room together.

I try to picture what August's face will look like. It's the face I used to know best. How will time have changed him? If I see him beforehand, will I be able to read his expression? Will he even try to communicate his intentions with me?

If he tells everyone that it was me who filed the patent, I will be seen as the avaricious antagonist who tried to catapult her husband into devastation. I've even brought the paperwork to prove the point. I will be taken from our daughter and face a life of imprisonment. This is what I am bracing myself for: a fate worse than death. I would be separated from my child and it is possible that she would never forgive me. I would never forgive myself.

But a small part of me can also see the catharsis that might happen if August tells the truth. I will be jailed, but I will finally be free.

And if he doesn't reveal my involvement, he will be taking the high road to protect me and our daughter, and only I will know that he is willing to destroy himself, as ever, for the greater good. Only I will know of his generosity, which makes it all the more generous. If this is what he does, I will feel gratitude, but no relief.

Do you see? No matter what he does, he will win.

AUGUST

Finally, it is morning. It's a grey one, though perhaps the heat of the August sun will burn through the veil of clouds yet. Time will tell, though I will not be here to see it: the courtroom has no windows.

My name is August Snow. I did everything you think I did, and I am innocent. If you do not think I am not innocent, then ask yourself: Is anyone?

I conceived of the nuclear chain reaction with pure intentions, and if it was used for evil, will you hold me accountable? A bomb is just an idea, and this is where its power lies. Everyone thinks it's in the destruction, but simply the thought of destruction is enough.

Along with my colleagues in the Chicago laboratories, we did everything we could to stop the use of the bomb in Japan.

We wrote to the President. We spoke on the radio. We organized petitions, marches. None of it did any good.

If it is the money that makes me guilty, then think of how many others in this world share in this guilt yet are rewarded for their actions, their greed. If it is the concept that makes me guilty, then consider: how many times have you had a bad thought which was never spoken aloud? Should you be punished for that? For thinking? A general, or a president, who has led a country to war, sacrificing the lives of countless soldiers and civilians—is he responsible for the blood on his hands? Only if he won, or only if he lost?

The ash falling from the sky is no longer visible. It might be that, just as when my eyes were the same colour as the sky, the dust is now the same colour as the fog, or it might be that the wake of the detonation has already settled.

I wonder what my brother thinks of all this. He's surely following the news, but, like everyone else, he has not written. I don't know him well enough anymore to know what this means, but I can imagine his shame. This is the only time that I've been glad for my father's death. He would be grateful, for the first and only time, that I no longer bear the same last name.

I wonder what it might have done for me, how things could have changed, had I believed in God as my parents did; if my understanding of the world had been formed by faith first, and science, evidence, and anything else, second.

My parents saw God as a cosmic force as well as a kind of omnibenevolent father, and they were quite happy living that way. I imagine that, if I'd believed in their God, there would be a degree of separation between myself and the immediate world. I can see how this might be a relief. I would not need to feel in control of things, or even responsible for them. It would mean that beauty would be appreciated first as the art of the divine, and secondly for the beauty of itself. Same for sorrow, for loss, for destruction. Would this instill in me a fear? A reverence? An acceptance of mystery that I have never been able to fathom, always wanting to find the answer, the *reason*, for all things? Would believing in God, and being a good Jew, have made me a better or worse scientist? A better or worse man? I'm not sure if it would bear any relevance to the former, only because I know many colleagues of mine who managed to be courageous and truthful scientists while still holding a strong religious conviction. I can see how it might have made me a lazier scientist, though, for there is always a way to dismiss mystery. But I do think faith would have made me a better husband, a better father. If nothing else, it would have made me feel less personally responsible for the events that shaped our lives, and for those that shaped the world at large, and I can see that this remove is what June longed for, for it might have allowed me to rein in my peripheral gaze to focus more narrowly on the present, on my family.

But even though I am not a man of God, I have nevertheless been persecuted for the faith into which I was born. And yet, I am still here. By some stroke of luck, I am still here.

I grieve for those who are not. I carry this grief the way I carry my identity. It wasn't hope so much as defiance that kept me going. Like a bomb, God is just an idea, and this is where the power lies.

I suppose I am thinking of all of this now because I feel as though I am approaching the end of my life, in a sense, and one often turns to God at the end. Would it be somehow *blasphemous*, of my beliefs, of my identity, to—well, truth be told, I feel rather alone, all of a sudden, and it might be nice to talk to someone who isn't here, who doesn't exist, to whom I owe nothing. It wouldn't do me any good to talk to anyone who knows me—no, not even to my memory of someone like my father. I want the neutral anonymity of a non-existent stranger. For the second time in my life (the first was when I converted to Christianity with my brother, to introduce myself to this new version of God, if nothing else) I feel like praying.

If I were to pray, I would say something like, Well, hello, it's me, August, August Snow. I might tell You something about how, though I'm beginning to feel quite nervous, with this feeling of walking down a dark hallway and all the doors closing as I pass by, shutting out all the remaining light, I still feel grateful for what I have seen of this world, and for the love I have known. I have had a good life. It could have been better, but that wasn't anyone's fault. I'm not blaming You, either. I'm not here to ask for anything. I just want some company in these last moments of the night. It's hardly even night anymore; had I slept, I would be waking now. I am watching the grey light of the day creep in, pushing away the

cloak of the Night Cockroach, every moment the pigmenta-
tion incrementally different until all of a sudden it is completely altered. It is dark, and then it is light. Watching the
sunrise is like watching someone age: you never notice it is
happening and then suddenly they are older, and you can't
remember what they looked like before any more than you
can remember what it was like to live in darkness. I can now
see the shapes of the trees and plants, the stone wall and mar-
gin of shoreline beyond it that was hidden under the cloak,
and in the sallow pallor of this dim morning. All the elements
appear to be a little disappointed not to be able to show off
their full colours, as if knowing it is the last morning that
I will be here to witness their display. By tonight I will be
placed in a different room, not a waiting room anymore, but
a decided room.

There's this line, maybe it's a saying, and it's been in my
head since I was a child. *Find what you love, and let it destroy you.*
Did You say that? Maybe it comes from one of the fairy tales
my mother read us, or maybe it's something that just came to
me, but over time, it has taken on the Biblical weight of truth.
It sounds dark, but it doesn't feel that way to me. I found what
I loved. June, and Leora.

Well, I think that's it. What are you supposed to say at the
end of a prayer? Thank you?

I change into my fresh clothes, chosen for the day and pressed
in advance. The socks are new. I brush my greying teeth and
comb out my grey curls. I've never thought so much about my

appearance and find it exhausting to have to be interested in such details.

I can hear someone walking down the hallway now, the footsteps even, solid. The percussive rhythm creates a bass note, steady, assured, and in my mind, in the long moments that stretch before me, I can hear a rumbling, the strings in the belly of the beginning of the movement tugging downwards, towards those flat, melancholy notes under which the melody of the flute lightly steps, meting out the sounds of warning, except it's no longer a warning, as it's too late.

I can see the face of the man who dropped me off here yesterday, and I associate the sounds of these footsteps with the same man, though there's no way I could know this for certain. This man was not the type to let emotion intervene with his work. He was gentle; moderate. Grey eyes, sombre face, the perfect posture of someone who is much stronger than they appear. When he arrives, he will unlock my door and lead me back down that same long, blank hallway to a room I have not yet seen, but I know exactly what to expect. I can see it in my mind. High ceilings, no windows, bright lights attempting to imitate daylight, wood panelling, and floors on which all shoes make echoes. This is the last room I will see as a free man. I do not feel nervous.

I imagine that June is there, sitting in the public gallery, and Leora too, by her side. I can see them, and I can feel the smile that will break my lips apart when I do. My instinct is always love. Leora will look so grown up but I know I will be able to see her baby self within. How could I not. Her eyes had settled into their final colour by the time I last saw her, so I will recognize those if nothing else: the deep, cobalt blue, like a memory, like a mirror. She looks so like my mother, and this gives me reassurance: time exists in a scale far beyond my own lifetime, and those that I love, those I have loved, remain on this earth, in some way, whether I am here or not.

Does she think of me as her father? Will seeing me evoke feelings of—I don't know—pride, and longing, and closeness? Or despair, disavowal? Did June bring her here simply to witness my downfall?

June will turn around when she hears the door opening; she will be able to recognize me by my footsteps alone, I am sure. Our eyes will meet, and she will know, as she has always known, exactly what I am thinking and feeling simply by looking at me. She will look beautiful. She always looks beautiful. I will nod to confirm her suspicions, and I will see the relief melt her shoulders down.

I have often wondered whether June had regrets. Whether she felt she acted rashly, in spite, and later wished she had considered the consequences, and how those consequences would implicate not just me, but the future of all of humanity. In other words, does she feel guilty?

It doesn't matter if I am guilty or not. People need something on which they can pin their blame. This is how our illogical minds try to comprehend, or create, logic. Everyone already believes me guilty whether they know the story or not. They see me as power-hungry, greedy, some lofty scientist bent on destruction who cares nothing for people. What will you think, now that you know the truth? It doesn't matter. I have failed in every way that I have tried to make my name or do what is right. I lost the people I love. I succeeded in creating the bomb, but I was unable to stop it from destroying me, and everyone else.

I could never let her take the fall. I would never take Leora's mother away from her. But me, I am already so far gone, it doesn't matter anymore.

I will get a message to June somehow. I've written it on a piece of paper that I am keeping in my pocket. *That paperwork I asked you to bring—I want you to destroy it. I asked you to bring it so that there would be no evidence for anyone to find. This is the end. You are free.*

I am innocent, I am guilty, I am human, and I will surrender.

TEN COMMANDMENTS

By Leó Szilárd, translated by Dr. Jacob Bronowski

1. Recognize the connections of things and the laws of conduct of men, so that you may know what you are doing.

2. Let your acts be directed towards a worthy goal, but do not ask if they will reach it; they are to be models and examples, not a means to an end.

3. Speak to all men as you do to yourself, with no concern for the effort you make, so that you do not shut them out from your world; lest in isolation the meaning of life slips out of sight and you lose the belief in the perfection of creation.

4. Do not destroy what you cannot create.

5. Touch no dish, except that you are hungry.

6. Do not covet what you cannot have.

7. Do not lie without need.

8. Honour children. Listen reverently to their words and speak to them with infinite love.

9. Do your work for six years; but in the seventh, go into solitude or among strangers, so that the recollection of your friends does not hinder you from being what you have become.

10. Lead your life with a gentle hand and be ready to leave whenever you are called.

AUTHOR'S NOTE

This is a work of fiction inspired by the lives of the twentieth-century inventor Leó Szilárd and his wife, Trude Weiss. The story is hung on certain historical facts of their lives, but many details have been changed. I was interested in exploring whether a person can be guilty for something they caused but did not intend to happen, and in my broad research for this very general theme I came upon Leó Szilárd and was immediately taken with his story. It seemed to me that this is what happened to him—his inventions became much larger than he was, and out of his control. As I read about his personal life, too, I wanted to explore the conflicts and complicities that might have been echoing in his marriage.

Many facts align with the novel: Leó Szilárd was a Hungarian scientist, and Trude Weiss was an Austrian professor of preventative medicine and a public health officer who worked in Colorado. They were both Jewish. Szilárd worked with Einstein in Berlin on the refrigerator and much more;

he conceived of nuclear chain energy in London; he soon realized the inevitability of the atomic bomb, giving his research to the American government to form the basis of the Manhattan Project. He was an ardent activist against the use of nuclear weapons: to that end, he created the Council for a Livable World, and was given the Atoms for Peace Award in 1959.

At a loss when the public wouldn't heed his calls to cease the nuclear arms race, Szilárd wondered whether people might listen to fiction instead. His collection of short stories is called *The Voice of the Dolphins*, and in that collection is a story called "My Trial as a War Criminal." This is where my idea for the completely fictionalized trial came from.

Some scenes and lines from this book come from letters Szilárd wrote; some come from his *Selected Recollections*, his deathbed memoirs dictated to Weiss; some come from his brother Bela's memoir, like the scene where August takes his brother to go see the elephants at the zoo.

The following books were the ones I turned to most: *Doomsday Men: The Real Dr Strangelove and the Dream of the Superweapon* by P. D. Smith; *Genius in the Shadows: A Biography of Leo Szilard, The Man Behind the Bomb* by William Lanouette with Bela Silard (Bela changed his last name from Szilárd); and *Leo Szilard: His Version of the Facts: Selected Recollections and Correspondence*, edited by Spencer R. Weart and Gertrud Weiss Szilard.

The character of Antonio is based on Enrico Fermi, who really did win the Nobel Prize for Physics alone for the work that Szilárd began.

Szilárd *did* invent the cobalt radiation machine (which is still the technology used for radiation treatment today), but he did so for use upon himself, to cure his own bladder cancer, *after* he had the idea for the cobalt bomb. Szilárd and Weiss were married, after many years of a long-distance relationship, but they never had children. Leora is pure invention: I created her to anchor some of the abstract themes in a very specific person, and because I had childhood cancer and am a mother, so these stories are the ones that live with me.

The Szilárd materials available for research, held in the public archives in the library of UC San Diego and digitized online, preserve only his side of the story. The materials were a vast and valuable resource, but included none of the return letters from Weiss. In his letters to her he was cruel, and cold. In real life, they were married until he died of a heart attack in his sleep, in 1964. Very little of Weiss's voice and life have been preserved in history, and in this void, my imagination had room to roam. From what I read she seemed like a victim in her marriage, and I wanted to imagine the ways in which she might have found her power.

THANK YOU TO:

Stephanie Sinclair, for believing in this book when it was only a seed of an idea; and Kelly Joseph, my brilliant and generous editor, for helping the seed to grow. I would not have believed in it, and therefore it would not exist, were it not for you. It continues to amaze me how many people are needed to produce a book, and I'm grateful to each and every person on the team at McClelland & Stewart who has been a part of bringing this book into the world. Paige Sisley, for your shepherding and insight that helped direct this novel in its final stages. Thank you to the Canada Council for the Arts and the Toronto Council for the Arts: time is money, so thank you for the gift of both. Damien Moule, for your historical and scientific knowledge — what luck, in writing this book, to have a friend who is a nuclear engineer with a deep knowledge of cobalt. Rosy Lamb: it was in conversation with you, while you painted me in your studio so many years ago, that I started thinking about these themes and characters. Seb Emina, for being interested in the stories I told and asking me to write about Leó Szilárd for *The Happy Reader* in 2015. Ingrid Smith and Nafkote Tamirat, for early reads and encouragement. Ashley Audrain, your support and correspondence means so much to me. My parents, Mary and David; it wasn't until I had children of my own that I understood how much you love me. A special thank you to my dad for his thorough, as ever, fact checking. To everyone who looked after, and loved, my children while I wrote, like Kyle, Omayya, Susan, Kaitlyn, Masha, Aidan. Arlo and Lucy, you are the sparks of my heart, thank you for rewriting my life. Cal Irvine, thank you for the ease with which you love; you are the anchor of our lives. And lastly, thank you to everyone who has ever read any of my books. To think of them, living in the world and in your minds, is sometimes too much for me; I am very grateful.

HARRIET ALIDA LYE is the author of the novel *The Honey Farm*, the memoir *Natural Killer*, and co-author of the picture book *Serge the Snail Without a Shell*. Her work has been published in the *New York Times*, the *Globe and Mail*, the *National Post*, *The Happy Reader*, *Hazlitt*, *Vice*, *Catapult*, and more. She lives in Toronto.